The Venom Versus Me

Look for these SpineChillers™

Dr. Shivers' Carnival of Terror
Attack of the Killer House
Pizza with Extra Creeps

SPINE CHILLERS™

The Venom
Versus Me

Fred E. Katz

THOMAS NELSON PUBLISHERS
Nashville • Atlanta • London • Vancouver

Published in Nashville, Tennessee, by Thomas Nelson, Inc., Publishers, and distributed in Canada by Word Communications, Ltd., Richmond, British Columbia. SpineChillers™ is a trademark of Thomas Nelson Publishers, Inc.

Editor: Lila Empson; Copyeditors: Nedra Lambert, Dimples Kellogg; Packaging: Kevin Farris, Belinda Bass; Production: Brenda White, Lori Gliko.

ISBN 0-7852-7480-4

Printed in the United States of America.

3 4 5 6 — 01 00 99 98 97 96

"Well, here we are," Dad announced between gasps. We stepped onto the front deck of what was to be our home for the next six weeks. His jeep looked like a toy on the tiny road below.

"Where? Top of Mount Everest?" I dropped my suitcase on the deck. *Crack!* It broke through a rotten plank. Teetering, it then fell sideways. "A perfect end to a perfect hike," I sputtered, blowing bangs off my hot forehead.

"Now, Brook." Dad lifted my long hair off my neck and slipped his arm around my shoulders. "You're missing the big picture, Hon. Just look at God's creation." He made a sweeping gesture, directing my attention to the surrounding mountaintops.

I had to nod. It was awesome. I had never been this high in any mountains before. It reminded me of the weekend our Sunday school class camped out near Connor's Bluff. But these mountains made those look like anthills.

1

"And just smell this air." He swelled his lungs dramatically.

"Please don't go Tarzan on me, okay? I'm not up to playing Boy. My lungs haven't kicked in since that last mile." I admit I'm the outdoor type, but I had never hiked such rugged terrain.

"Pure unpolluted oxygen at last," Dad said, seemingly ignoring my point.

"Oh really? What about that tourist traffic we left down in the village? Where do you think those fumes go?"

Again, Dad ignored my comment. "Why, we can even sleep with our windows open, Brook. Fresh mountain air will wake us each morning."

I picked up my suitcase. "Not to mention bears, cougars, or anything else that likes the flavor of sleeping tourists."

"Now there you go. You promised you would work on your negativity."

I sighed as I wrestled the screen door open. "You're right. This is kind of cool, especially the way those birds are soaring down there. Hawks?"

Dad turned to look, then sucked in his breath. "Eagles, Brook." His voice was hushed. "Real honest-to-goodness eagles."

"Really?" We stood there for a moment, watching as two eagles gracefully sailed in front of the golden sunset, then banked and plummeted behind a cliff.

For a moment I almost forgot where I was and my

mission: to be my dad's "baby-sitter" for the next six weeks, hidden away in some mountain chalet.

Did I say mountain chalet? Well, that's what the brochure called it. But to me it looked more like Abe Lincoln's log cabin on stilts. And talk about isolated. I mean, where was everybody anyway? We had not passed a single cabin—excuse me, chalet—for miles.

The cabin was okay on the inside, though. There was a phone, and there was a rustic fireplace at one end of the living room. A tiny kitchen was hidden behind the wooden stairs that led to the loft.

"Oh, what a shame," I moaned, leaning on the kitchen doorjamb. "The kitchen's too small. I guess we're forced to take our meals down in the village."

"And scarf down tons of fat?" Dad was already climbing to the loft. "No way. We'll just cook in there and eat out by the fireplace."

I had to smile. "*We?* Remember, I volunteered to do the cooking while we're here." Dad was an excellent cook, but he needed to devote his time to studying. He agreed to let me do the cooking if I stuck to his low-fat diet plan.

Ever since his brother died suddenly of a heart attack, he'd become gung ho about "stripping fats" from everything. That meant no pizza with "the works," no hamburgers and greasy French fries, no lasagna dripping with cheese.

This was Dad's big summer. In six weeks he would

be a lawyer, provided this retreat up the lonely mountain gave him enough time to prepare for his exams.

To be a lawyer had been a ten-year dream of his. Raising a family had postponed it until now.

And that's where you come in, Brook, I thought to myself. I would make sure he didn't get distracted from studying so he would be ready to blister that bar exam.

Oh, well, I thought. *I better check out my own bedroom. I hope it's larger than this Barbie-goes-camping kitchen.*

"Where do you think our nearest neighbors live?" I called, stopping to check an odd design carved in the doorjamb. Looking like a big coiled snake with feathers around its throat, the design held my attention . . . and gave me the creeps.

"In caves."

"Cute, Dad. I mean really."

"Seriously, Brook. This mountain range is chock full of caves, some very historic. The Tocagons called them *atsi.*"

"Thanks for the lesson on Native Americans, but I mean it. Where is the next chalet?" I surveyed my new room, dust, broken window, and all. There was one dresser, one bed, and a leaning night table.

"Not for miles, I hope. You know I've got to have quiet for my exam cram."

I ran my hand across the dresser coated with dust. *Hey, what's this?* I spied an emblem scrawled in the

4

dust. It was the same as the one carved on the door-jamb. I smudged the dust out quickly.

Just some foolish prank by a former renter, I decided. They should've been spending their time cleaning. But the truth was, it looked like no one had lived in here for years.

"You're not afraid up here, are you?"

I threw my suitcase on the bed. Uh-oh. I knew I shouldn't have asked about neighbors. "Of course not, Dad. It's just that I may want to borrow a cup of candy bars every now and then."

"Well," he continued, "you know I'd prefer you to stay with me at the library. It'd be fun. You can catch up on reading, and we could have lunch together every day—"

"Dad!" This was the zillionth time we had been over this subject. My summer spent indoors? No way.

"Okay, okay, but I still don't like you staying up on this mountain alone. One hint of a problem and I'll have to arrange something better. I mean it."

Arrange? I straightened my back. That word smacked of baby-sitting. "Get serious. I'm twelve years old and almost as tall as you and Mom." I flipped a strand of hair behind my ear. It snagged on my loop earring.

"I know there are some kids around here somewhere." *Unless the bears have eaten them,* I thought to myself. "Just give me a day or two, okay?"

5

The bumping overhead told me he was unpacking his computer. "Well, you do have Bratwurst."

I laughed as I unpacked my clothes. Bratwurst was our longhaired dachshund. He was about as protective as an attack goldfish.

Suddenly it hit me. *Brat. Where is Brat?* The last time I saw him he was sniffing around the front porch.

"Here Brat!" I called, as I unpacked my T-shirts and opened the bottom drawer of the dresser. "Come on, boy. I'm back—"

I froze. There in the shadows of the drawer I saw something move. A long, cylindrical mass began to slither and twist upon itself, working its way into a coil.

At first I couldn't move. Then I took a few steps back. I finally lunged for the bedroom door, almost tripping over Brat.

Get out! a voice inside me urged. *Get out!*

I scooped up a bewildered Brat and ran toward the front door.

"Brook?" Dad's voice was questioning. "What's going on down there?"

I squatted under a tree and cradled Brat in my arms. I was still trembling, remembering that huge snake coiled in my drawer. My hand had been so close to it. And hadn't I heard the whirring of the snake's warning rattle? Just the thought made my breath rev up again.

Come on, Brook, I thought. *Get a grip. Dad's going to wonder what you're doing out here in the yard.* And telling him my room housed an angry rattlesnake was the last thing I'd ever do. One hint and he'd lock me in that library forever.

I let go of Brat.

"Hey," Dad called from the upper window. I jumped a mile. "No fair goofing off. We've got lots to do yet."

I stood up and waved to him. *Like chasing a rattlesnake out of my room,* I thought, dreading having to go back in that shadowy room. I was beginning to be uneasy about this place with its carvings and gruesome guest.

In the kitchen I found a heavy broom and a wide dustpan with a sharp edge. I could use the dustpan as field, I decided, creeping down the short hall. I made Brat stay outside. The huge rattlesnake already seemed agitated enough.

Slowly, I crept into my room. My heart was racing. I forced my gaze down to the open drawer.

Nothing but shadows.

On tiptoe with broom poised, I stepped forward, inch by inch, until I was practically hovering over it.

I peered into the drawer.

"Gone!" The word slipped out. The rattlesnake had disappeared! I lowered the broom, more confused than relieved.

Then it hit me. *Gone . . . or just hiding?* I swirled around and scanned my tiny bedroom.

Is it under the bed?

In my closet?

Under my pillow?

The thought of a loose poisonous snake in my room made my legs go shaky. I sank down on my bed, and then jumped up with a start—it could even be under the mattress!

I groaned. "That snake could be hiding anywhere!"

"Brook?"

"Yessir?"

"When you have a break, come up here and help me set up my computer, okay?"

"Coming!" I was already out the door heading toward the loft. I was never so glad to do slave labor in my life. After all, snakes would never climb the rickety staircase, I assumed, as I ran up by twos. And I never needed to be so close to Dad in my whole life.

While I helped him with the computer, I began asking questions about snakes. I kept it cool, though, telling him about a movie I had seen once. There had been a snake hiding in a gold miner's cabin and he never could track it down.

"Well, I doubt if that miner had just one snake to worry about," Dad said as he connected the cables. "Most snakes travel in pairs."

Oh, great, I thought. *There could be two rattlesnakes hiding in my room?* "But why would snakes stay around people anyway?"

"Warmth."

I stood still. "Warmth?"

"Snakes are cold-blooded creatures. They seek warmth from humans, especially at night. Snakes have even been found curled up in people's clothes." He turned. "Did you say the miner lived in the desert?"

"Huh? Oh, yes, the desert." My thoughts were whirling.

"Hey, why the big interest in snakes? I thought just a picture of one turned you to Jell-O." We had finished setting up the computer, and Dad began to unpack his gear.

I faked a smile. "For sure. But it was an okay movie. I . . . I was just wondering." I ran my hand across his shoulder. "So how about a glass of tea?"

"Thanks, but no. Let's whip this place in order

9

before nightfall." He threw me his zipper bag. "Then we can call tomorrow our own."

I agreed, grateful that we could work together.

But nightfall turned out to be more like 10:00 P.M. We were worn out by then. Dad made a fire in the fireplace, and we collapsed in front of it.

Our dinner turned out to be the snacks I had bought on the road. I had stuffed my purse full. They would be my survival kit while trapped on a mountain with a health nut.

"I've got a few M&M's left." I rolled off my stomach and offered them. "They make a great dessert after a bag of corn chips and peanut butter crackers."

He reached for them sheepishly. "Some example I am—zero willpower."

"Don't worry. One meal of junk food won't hurt."

I lay on my back, listening to the crackle of the fire. The fireplace provided the only light in the cabin. Gazing at the darkened ceiling, I began to relax.

Dad leaned back on his elbows, watching the shadows flicker against the log wall. "Just listen to that."

I stiffened. "What?" My pulse quickened.

"That's just it—nothing. The sound of silence."

"Oh." I exhaled a sigh of relief. "It is nice, in an eerie sort of way."

Suddenly Brat jumped to his feet and began barking his warning bark.

"What's wrong, fella?"

He ran frantically from the door to the window.

10

I grabbed my flashlight and went to the window. I peered through the upper pane.

"See anything?"

"No, just the outline of trees and—hey!" I ran to the door, Brat still barking like crazy. "Hey, who's out there?"

"Hurry!" Dad hissed, pushing me toward the kitchen.

"What?" I demanded. "What did you see?"

He didn't answer. But the look on his face said it wasn't Mickey Mouse. "I don't like this," he muttered as we crept out the back door. "Not one bit!"

I reached down for Brat, but he had disappeared into the moonless night. "Here, boy," I whispered.

"Shhh!"

I grew silent. I had never seen Dad so uptight. *What had he seen in our front yard?*

"Brook?"

"Dad?"

"You stay right here. Understand?"

"Can't I at least go down the steps?"

"Brook!" It was his bottom-line, serious voice.

"Okay, okay. But where are you going?"

He nodded to the right.

"Around to the front?" I squinted to see his face in the dark. "But why? Why not through the—"

He gripped my arm. "Listen, Hon. If you hear

anything—I mean *anything*—you start running, okay?"

Something in his voice frightened me. It sounded like he was saying a kind of good-bye.

"NO!" I protested. "I'm going with you." I reached for his hand and squeezed it.

He squeezed back. "You heard me. Any noise and you start running. Then circle around toward the back road." He paused and sucked in his breath. "Spend the night in the woods if necessary. You'll find the road better by daylight. Then flag down some tourists. They'll—"

"Stop it! You're scaring me. What noise? What are you talking about?"

He slipped down the steps. "Gunshots," he whispered from below. "If you hear any gunshots."

I stiffened. *Gunshots?* "But you don't have a gun." I stumbled down the steps.

"True. But they do." And with that he was gone. Only his words hung in the night air.

I stood there, helpless and completely alone. I couldn't even see where he had gone. All I knew was, he was unarmed, yet warning me that "they" had guns. What's more, I was to run if I heard any shots.

All at once my body turned into an icicle. But I also knew what I had to do. There was no way I was going to let Dad face some gun alone.

I looked around, then I half ran toward some towering trees. *At least I can help him by surprising our intruders.* I ran my hand across the scrubby ground, feeling for any fallen limbs. In the dark a thick limb could look like a rifle or at least look frightening—I hoped. I could help Dad that much. But as I ran my hand blindly over the forest floor the thought of the escaped rattlesnake crept across my mind.

I cringed. That creature could be out here in the dark just waiting for my outstretched hand.

Yipes!

I jumped back, grabbing my hand. What was that cold, wet thing? Suddenly something was jumping at my knees, whimpering.

"Brat?" I whispered, reaching down. "Is that you?" But he was already jumping as high as my waist. "Good boy." I scooped him up gratefully. At least one member of my family was safe, wet nose and all.

I squeezed him tightly. "Still, Brat," I said quietly into his fur. "Be still." I waited until I felt his soft body relax. "Good boy."

I eased him slowly onto the ground. I just had to find something to defend Dad with . . . and me, too.

Suddenly the phone rang.

I jolted upright. I ran back up the steps. Dad said the rental people had promised to connect the phone by the weekend. I grabbed the screen door. *Whoever that is can help like crazy.*

"Hello!" I practically screamed.

There was a pause. "Brook?"

"Mom!"

14

"Honey, what's wrong?"

I swallowed slowly. *Get a grip*, I told myself. This was Mom, hundreds of miles away. There was no reason to make her frantic. What help could she be anyway? "Oh . . . oh, nothing."

"Brook." It was her come-clean-with-me voice.

"No, Mom, I mean it. Brat just startled me, that's all." I was glad that much was true. "He's been playing tricks. You know how he is."

She didn't say anything. I knew she was testing my tone of voice. "Okay," she said finally. "So you two are settled in?"

I assured her we were. As I was talking, I tried to stretch the cord over to the front window.

"Let me talk to your dad."

"Sure, but he's . . . outside right now."

"At this time of night? Don't tell me your chalet doesn't have plumbing."

I had to laugh. *Plumbing?* Dad was out there somewhere in the dark getting ready to confront someone with a gun, and Mom was worried about *plumbing*? "Oh, yes, we have everything," I told her. Including a rattlesnake and night intruders!

Then Dad appeared at the back door. "You shouldn't be so close to that window, Brook. Get down."

I put my hand over the receiver. "It's Mom."

His shoulders slumped. "You didn't tell her—"

"No way. But she wants to talk to you."

He looked at the receiver, hesitated, then grabbed

15

it. "Honey, listen. I'm right in the middle of something. Can I call you back?"

She must have reminded him I had said he was outside. His brow wrinkled.

"I've got to take care of something. I'll call you right back, okay? All right. Good-bye."

"Way to go," I said when he hung up.

"I just hope I did the right thing, not telling her." His face was too serious to calm me. "But we better get this over with." He moved toward the door. "That phone ruined my plan to surprise them."

I went over to Dad. Whoever was on the other side of that door would have to face us together.

Two strangers, a man and a teenage boy, stood in the cabin doorway. "Hush!" I warned Brat, who had backed up against me.

"Sorry we took you by surprise," said the man. He wore a plaid jacket and logging boots and held a shotgun by its muzzle.

"Yeah," the boy added. He looked to be about sixteen. "You weren't what we were expecting to find either. Right, Dad?"

The man nodded. "Nick, you better go check on your sister. She was supposed to stick close behind us."

Sister? My heart thumped. The boy turned around and took a few steps away from the doorway, shining his flashlight into the dark night.

Dad eyed the man like a detective. "What exactly was it you were expecting to find around our cabin?"

"A bear," the man answered matter-of-factly. "We had trailed him as far as that ravine yonder. He's a mean one. Already mauled two deer."

17

"A bear?" I blurted out. I looked at Dad, who was still scrutinizing the burly stranger.

"Yes. He's been prowling around our trailer every night this week."

"There you are, Sandi!" the boy called. He stepped back into the doorway, accompanied by a slender girl.

The girl looked at me rather shyly. "Hi. We had no idea somebody lived here. Otherwise we—"

"Yeah," the boy interrupted. "Who'd have thought they'd ever rent this unit out."

Dad didn't seem to hear this unsettling comment, but I did.

"Let's get back to this roaming bear, okay?" Dad's jaw had a determined set. "Were you going to shoot it? I thought firearms were forbidden in this area of the mountain range."

The man seemed impressed with Dad's knowledge of the law. He continued to explain that he had no intention of shooting the bear, unless his life was in danger. He was only tracking it. Then he could report it to the mountain rangers. "They can't afford to let that rascal roam. Hey, we better introduce ourselves. I'm Chad Ponder and these are my kids, Nick and Sandi."

After Dad introduced us, the three guys soon got into a big discussion on the habits of wild bears.

But I was more interested in Sandi. She looked to be about twelve or thirteen. She had big green eyes and long, reddish-brown hair. I liked the way she smiled a lot. After a day like mine, I could use a few smiles.

"You been here long?" I asked as she came over by the fire.

"Too long. Dad's a contractor. He and my brother are surveying this area of the mountains." She held her palms toward the flame. "It takes weeks to complete."

I asked her where they were staying. She pointed behind our cabin.

"You mean you climb this mountain every day?"

"Oh, no, not you, too!" She laughed. "Didn't the rental people tell you? There's a back road. It cuts the climb by half."

"Well, that news calls for a celebration. Let's go to the kitchen and have some iced tea."

But my cheerful mood vanished as I recalled the incident with the rattlesnake. I felt I had to confide in someone, so I told Sandi about finding a rattlesnake in the drawer. I also told her about the strange design on the doorjamb.

"Did your dad kill the snake?"

I yanked open the refrigerator door. "No. The snake was gone when I went back to my room. Dad doesn't even know about it."

"You're kidding."

I then told her that my dad needed time to study and I didn't want to worry him. "Besides, he's just waiting for a reason to make me do time indoors at the library."

"A rattler, you say?"

I handed her a glass of tea. "I'm pretty sure that's what it was. I didn't get a close look at it, but I know it was big, and I saw it twist into a coil. And I thought I heard a rattle."

"Can I tell my brother?"

I shrugged. "Can he keep secrets?"

"Nick *is* a secret. Dad and I try to keep him locked in the closet, but he keeps slipping through the keyhole."

I laughed. *Yeah, I like this girl,* I decided.

But when she called Nick, he didn't seem so cool. In fact, when she told him about my visitor, he shot her a worried glance.

She ignored him.

"See!" he said. "I told you I was right! I—"

But Nick didn't have time to finish because his sister gave his hip a bump. "Don't pay any attention to him. He reads too much. Then he can't separate what he reads from the real world."

"Cut it out, Sandi. These folks have a right to—"

"To sleep," she interjected quickly, pulling him by the arm back into the front room. "Come on, Dad, it's late. Let's aim this guy down the mountain." She got behind her brother, bulldozer-style.

As Nick and Mr. Ponder headed toward the door, Sandi sidled over. "Don't let my brother worry you," she whispered. "There were other reasons we turned this cabin down—not just the legend."

I looked at her, wide-eyed. "What legend?" Then I paused. "You were going to have this cabin first?"

"I'll stop by tomorrow, okay?" She waved her hand over her head. "But be ready for a hike to the village."

"Yeah . . . fine." I stood there in a daze as the Ponders stepped out into the moonlight.

Dad said he was bone tired and needed to get some sleep. Once he was up in the loft, I urged Brat to follow me to my room. Surely if the snake returned, Brat would sense it and give a warning bark.

After shaking out my nightshirt, I checked under the bed, the mattress, and both pillows. *So far so good,* I decided, and jumped into bed, glad to get my feet off the floor.

After much hesitation, I finally turned off the table lamp and lay there in the dark. The only sound was Brat's even breathing and a limb scratching against the broken pane.

How did that rattlesnake ever get in my closed drawer? And what about that strange carving of a snake. Was it just a coincidence?

I rolled over. I didn't want to think about that now. *Maybe tomorrow,* I thought as I tried to turn off my mind. I slapped my hands over my ears and said a silent prayer. I willed myself to relax. And after a while it seemed to be working. I even burrowed deeper into my pillow.

Then I heard it. I wanted to sit up and turn on the light, but I was frozen with fear. No! I wanted to scream. *No!*

The sound of the death rattle was as distinct as Brat's steady breathing. My heart pounded in my chest. The snake was out there in the dark, coiled and ready to spring.

I felt something cold and moist against my cheek. It moved to my chin, and then to my neck. I jerked and let out a gasp. My eyelids flew open to see Brat nuzzling against my face, his cold, moist nose pressing against my ear.

The room was dimly illuminated now by the early morning light filtering through the window. *I must have fallen asleep,* I mused wearily, trying to clear my head. *But when? Did I only dream I heard the death rattle?*

I rubbed my eyes and looked around the room, then down at the floor. *Nothing unusual here.* There were no unusual sounds either, just the chirping of birds outside the window and the thud of Dad's footsteps overhead.

I stepped onto the floor and over to the dresser. I cautiously opened the bottom drawer and peered inside. Nothing there but T-shirts. I grabbed some clothes, let Brat outside, then made my way to the shower before dressing and heading to the kitchen to cook our breakfast.

"Hi!"

I jumped a foot. "Oh, hi!" I said, breathless, staring at Sandi. She was sitting on our porch step. The early sun was playing on the red in her hair.

"Sorry I scared you. I saw your dad leave. So I thought I'd sit out here till you were through with breakfast stuff."

I joined her on the step. "I'd rather stay out here, believe me."

I nudged her knee. "I had a nightmare last night. I dreamed I heard the death rattle, that the snake was coiled somewhere in my room."

"Eerie. But at least it was just a dream."

"Yeah. I mean, it must have been a dream. But it seemed so real. You know, you really had me scared last night."

"Me?" She leaned back on her elbows. "How come?"

"All that stuff about not renting our chalet. You acted pretty spooked about it. And you practically shoved your brother out the door when he was saying he knew something about our rattlesnake."

She scoffed. "Forget Nick. He's a walking encyclopedia. He'll tell you anything."

"He sounded pretty serious to me."

"Did you tell your dad about the rattlesnake yet?"

24

I assured her I hadn't.

She sat there for a moment. Then she said, "Maybe you better. These mountain snakes aren't at all cowards. Some even go in search of victims."

I let out a nervous laugh. "You're really a big help, Sandi."

"But I'm serious. You really shouldn't stay in there alone if a rattler is on the prowl."

"Do you think there could be some connection between the rattler, the strange carving, and the image traces in the dust?"

"Come on," she said. "Let's take that hike into the village. I think I know someone who can answer your question."

Sandi and I set out toward the back road, the shortcut the rental agents forgot to tell Dad and me about. On the way to the village, Sandi told me a little about herself. She said her mother had died a year ago, and this had been especially tough on her. She said her mother had always been her best friend and that she never made friends easily at school. "I guess I'm just too shy," she added.

"Well, you've just made one tight friend," I said. "By the way, don't keep me in suspense. Who is this person you think I should meet?"

"Sister Howling Wind."

"Sister who?"

"Howling Wind. Hey, pick up the pace. We've got to get there and back before sunset."

Sandi began to walk faster and I worked to keep up with her, wondering all the while what I was getting myself into.

We reached the village and approached a circle of tents. We made our way inside the circle, and instantly the hair on the back of my neck rose up. *This is spooky,* I thought as I glanced around.

Dozens of people sat stone-faced around a fire. The flames cast eerie shadows on the tents. I sensed an air of expectancy. No one said a word. The only sound was the thunder rumbling in the distance.

After we sat down in the circle, I leaned over to Sandi. "Who did you say I was going to meet?" I whispered.

"Sister Howling Wind. She's one of the last surviving members of the Tocagon tribe. She gives these lectures to tourists about her people."

I shook my head. "Is that supposed to mean something to me?"

Sandi turned to look at me, her eyes reflecting the flames. "It will. Shhh . . . here she comes."

Suddenly the tent flap raised. A thin, elderly woman wearing an animal-hide tunic stepped out. Although her back was bent, she stepped gingerly, her sharp eyes surveying the group.

"Kwai-chiumin," she said as she lowered herself down by the fire.

The crowd remained silent.

"That is the greeting of my people," she announced, passing both palms over the flames. "The people of these mountains, the *first* people of these mountains, the Tocagons." She then said something, cast a pinch

27

of dirt into the fire, and raised her arms skyward, chanting.

Sandi and I exchanged glances.

"But now my people have gone the way of the mountain cougar." She looked around, her eyes piercing. "And all because of one brave's disobedience."

She continued to tell how the Tocagons once numbered in the hundreds. "There were settlements all over this mountain range. All except for the *kontai,* of course. No one dared live close to the *kontai.*"

Everyone looked at one another. We waited for Sister Howling Wind to explain this word. But she moved on.

"Then when I was still eating gruel from my mother's bowl, there came a great fever. It had not touched our people, but the Allendir tribes were suffering." She pointed toward the east. "They live beyond the mountains.

"My father was the medicine man for our village, so he agreed to go to help them. My mother and other women also went to help with the sick." She paused, her gaze dropping to the flames. "She took me, too."

She then said that after many days they returned to the home mountains. They found the village untouched, but not one of the Tocagons was alive.

"Not one," she repeated, as she gazed into the flames again. "Not one."

"An enemy tribe?" offered a man sitting near her.

She cut her eyes toward him. He shrank back.

"The Tocagons were peace-loving." She held her palms toward the flames. "We had no enemies." Her gaze grew distant. "Not any outside our own campfires, at least."

The poor man looked like he was going to apologize, but she held one bony hand up. He remained silent.

She then explained that she and some of the other women weren't the only survivors. Some braves had also been away with a small foraging party looking for food. They, too, came home to find their tribespeople dead. "It was they who held the answer."

I waited, breathless. We all waited.

But Sister Howling Wind sat quietly for a moment, lost in thought, before she continued.

"Our people, you see, believed in the natural order of this world. Every living thing has borders. To step beyond one's border is to invite evil." Her thin face became sunken.

"The son of our chief was the one. He brought us destruction from the evil Upshan. He and his pride."

Upshan? Who was Upshan? After all, she said her people didn't have any enemies. So he couldn't be some rival tribal leader.

"The great Upshan was . . . *is* a giant serpent," she explained. "He lived in these mountains long before the first Tocagon. As long as a mountain pine is tall, he rules his mountain—he and his clan, the Night-Twisters. They are his messenger serpents."

She then told us how the young Tocagon brave had

tried to prove his valor. He had dared to approach Upshan's mountain home. The surviving party had heard him boast of his plan.

"When we returned," she concluded, "we found the great serpent with scarlet and lavender feathers had made his strike . . . true to his warning signs."

She cast another pinch of dirt into the fire, then rose to her feet.

"So, for one act of disobedience our whole tribe was destroyed." She turned toward the entrance to her tent. "Such can be the consequence when one grows too bold."

She turned and looked at us. "Such can be the consequence when one angers the mighty feathered Upshan."

A chill went down my spine. *Feathered?* Did she say Upshan was a feathered serpent? The image on my doorjamb flashed through my mind. I looked at Sandi.

"I thought you might be interested," she whispered.

"Come on. You look like you could stand a cold drink."
Sandi pulled my sleeve.

I balked. I wasn't interested in a soda. What I wanted was to sort things out in my mind. That eerie old woman stirred up too many scary questions.

"Brook." Sandi waved her hand before my eyes. "Earth to Brook."

"Okay, I give. Where can we get a drink?"

Sandi led us to a corner shop that looked new. It had mountain souvenirs on one side and a few tables on the other. We selected a table by the counter.

"Okay, name your poison," Sandi announced. "It's my treat."

"I love your choice of words."

Sandi laughed. "Oh, yeah. Okay, scratch 'poison' and add 'favorite float.'"

"Hi, Sandi!" We turned to see a heavy man with horn-rimmed glasses behind the counter.

"Hey, there, Mr. Johnson," she called. "What happened to your regular counter boy?"

Mr. Johnson ran a cloth across the counter. "Guess he caught the bug, too. So I'm my own soda jerk these days."

Sandi turned in her swivel chair. "Bug?"

The man shrugged. "Well, I don't have to tell you what's happened to my other help. They start out eager to please, then hear about this place and disappear."

Sandi cut her gaze toward me. It seemed to say I wasn't supposed to hear that. "Oh, what do they know? You'll get somebody soon."

He leaned forward. "Which brings me to my usual question—"

She held up her hand. "Sorry, Mr. Johnson. I've got a job, remember? It's called keeping my dad and Nick straight."

"But the hours would be flexible and you wouldn't have to come in till noon."

Sandi shook her head.

"Okay," he muttered. "But, hey, who's your friend there?"

Sandi introduced us, then said, "She's here on family duty, too."

The owner looked at me. "What do you say? Would you like a summer job?"

Sandi was giving me every negative expression she had.

"I don't know." I fidgeted with the menu. "I mean, I can't now. Maybe in a week or two?"

"Great! You just let me know. Now, what will you girls have?"

We gave him our order and he began to draw our drinks.

Sandi leaned forward. "Don't encourage him," she whispered.

I leaned in. "Why? If Dad threatens to take me to the library every day, I could always save my sanity by working here."

Sandi sat back, exasperated. "You and this place would be the worst possible mix. Talk about 'poison'!"

"What's the problem, anyway? It looks like a cool place to me."

"Yeah, right. I mean, it's okay now, but, well, let's not ruin a perfectly good afternoon, okay?"

I wanted to ask her what she meant, but I thought I'd sample my float first. While we drank, some tourists came in and milled around the souvenir tables. Then a loud clap of thunder brought a dozen people scurrying in from the sidewalk.

Suddenly a guy in a yellow jacket picked up a plastic doll in Native American dress. "Maybe this dude is the weather villain!" he shouted to a buddy. "Maybe he did a rain dance or something!" They both laughed.

"Put that down!"

Everyone in the shop turned to see Mr. Johnson roaring around the counter. His face was fire-engine red. "Go take your big mouth somewhere else!"

The guy and his friend stood, dumbfounded. "Hey,

I didn't mean anything. Honest. And the doll's not broken."

"Out!" Mr. Johnson shouted. *"Out!"*

Not only did the two guys slip out, but so did most of the embarrassed witnesses, including Sandi and me. She nudged me toward a covered bench.

"What was that all about?"

Sandi tucked one foot under her. "See. You don't want to work back there."

"Not if the boss is crazy. Does he blow up like that often?"

"He's not crazy, Brook. Just maxed out."

I leaned back. "Oh, you mean the people who keep quitting on him. That's just a bunch of bad breaks."

She lifted her hair from her neck. "Not exactly. It's just that they stay around long enough to hear about his streak of bad luck, then take off."

"What bad luck?"

"It's really some kind of problem with the property. See, Mr. Johnson just bought this place last spring. It hadn't even been rebuilt yet."

"Rebuilt?" I propped one leg up. "What happened?"

She told how the original owner had had a good business, selling snacks and mountain souvenirs. "Then he got greedy. He decided to sell plastic versions of the legendary Upshan. Sister Howling Wind and some of the other Native Americans warned him that he was playing with fire. Um, so to speak."

34

"Hold it!" I sat forward. "Don't tell me the whole place just disappeared, owner and all."

"Worse. The first week he began to sell the toy replicas, his store was struck by—get this—purple lightning! Burned to the ground in minutes."

I shook my head. "No way."

"Okay, Brook. Don't buy it. But there were three witnesses that night. And none was Native American."

I sat there, thinking about that son of the chieftain Sister Howling Wind told about. He had angered the feathered serpent and the village had suffered for his boldness. Now Sandi was telling about another man who seemed to have angered the ancient Upshan and lost his whole business.

Like a tidal wave, I felt a sudden longing to be by myself. I needed to go home and think all these things out. If what I was hearing was true, what could be in store for me?

That evening, back at the cabin, I pondered Sister Howling Wind's story. Either the carving of a feathered serpent on my doorjamb was some cruel joke, or I was in serious trouble.

If her story was true, the rattlesnake in my room may not have been just a coincidence.

And what about Sandi? She must sense something very strange about this chalet. Otherwise, why would the Ponders turn it down?

I rolled over on my bed, socking my pillow. *Well, at least I haven't heard the warning rattle of our hidden snake tonight,* I thought, praying that it had finally slithered away.

"Brook!"

I was jolted awake. The sun was streaming across my pillow. *Oh, no! I'm late and Dad's got to get to the library.*

"Here we are." Dad stepped into my room. His

briefcase was serving as a breakfast tray. "Toast, scrambled eggs, and fresh fruit."

I smiled. "I'm sorry, Dad. I should've set my alarm."

He sat down on the bed, handing me a plate. "What's a dad for if he can't treat his daughter."

I looked at my plate. It really did look delicious. "Thanks, Dad. I'm starving."

He told me this was to celebrate the good news.

"Good news? I can sure use some."

"The rangers caught the scavenger bear. Things should be back to normal now."

I swallowed a sputter. *Normal?* "I sure hope so. Not that I was worried," I quickly added, afraid he might still find someone to stay with me. "Sandi's teaching me a lot about this area."

This pleased him. After breakfast we had our morning devotional, then he dashed down to his jeep. He said he wanted to claim a good study nook before the library filled up for morning story hour.

After Dad left, I put on an Amy Grant CD and flipped through some magazines. But nothing snagged my interest. So I decided to make Dad's favorite meat loaf. Of course, I had to use ground turkey instead of ground beef to cut down on the fat. But, after all, he deserved it. I'd even add chives to his low-fat mashed potatoes.

Heading out to the kitchen, I passed that wretched carving again. There it was—a broad-headed serpent, coiled, with feathers bristling around its throat. "I can't take this!" I said out loud. Then I got an idea—I'd tape a piece of paper over it.

There! I thought, giving the tape one last blow with my fist. Snake, gone.

No sooner had I tucked the tape in my jeans than I heard scratching sounds out front.

I shuddered. "Who's there?"

No answer. But the scratching got louder.

"Brat? Is that you?"

The loud scratching now became frantic.

I ran to the front room.

I tiptoed up behind Brat. "Come on, fella. Let Brook see." I held out my hand. He ran from me.

"Bratwurst!" I used my command voice.

His ears drooped. But he did stop. *Klunk.* Something fell from his mouth.

"Good boy." I reached down and scratched behind his ears. "What've you got here?" I stared at the object. It certainly was not a bone. I rolled it over with the toe of my shoe.

"Wow!" I knelt down to get a closer look. It was an odd-looking stone. It was black, round, and smooth, but its center mesmerized me. In its depths flashed bright deep red and purple fires, almost as though they were electric or something.

I reached out to touch it, but something held me back.

"Where did you get this, boy?"

Brat wagged his tail.

I looked at it again. It was alive with lightning bolts of color. Then something kicked at the back of my thoughts. *Deep red and purple.* Why did those colors ring a bell with me?

Then I caught myself. *Hey! What's going on here? This is just some silly rock, right? Why am I so uptight about a stone my dog drags in?* I bent over and grasped the stone.

"Yuck!" I dropped it immediately. Not only was it cold and clammy to the touch, but it seemed to be, well, alive. I mean it throbbed, sort of. *Now your imagination is really working overtime, Brook,* I reasoned.

Rubbing my hands down my jeans, I stepped back and stared at it. *What kind of stone is this anyway?*

"Knock, knock."

My heart pounded as I swirled on my heels.

Sandi was squinting through the screen door. "Anybody home?"

I ran to the door and practically dragged her in. "I could hug you, Sandi Ponder!"

She laughed. "Wow, I didn't think I was that terrific." She paused. Something about my expression made her grow serious. "Brook, are you okay?"

I nodded. "No, I mean, well, okay, sort of, but—"

"Hold it, girl. Take a deep breath and sit down over here. Then when your brain recharges, tell me everything." She aimed me toward the sofa. "Hey, what's this?" She leaned down to pick up the strange stone.

"No!" I shouted.

Startled, she bolted upright.

I quickly apologized, explaining how it got there. She scrutinized it closely but never touched it. "It is weird. Beautiful, but weird. Just look at those flashes of color."

"Exactly. Does that remind you of anything?"

Her chin tilted. "No, not a—hey, wait a minute." She looked at me. "No-o-o, it wouldn't have any connection."

"See. You thought about it, too. Sister Howling Wind said Upshan's feathers were—"

"Scarlet and lavender," she said, looking down at the strange object again. "We need to get this to Nick. He'll know what it is."

I got up. "But how? I'm not touching it again. It . . . it looks spooky to me and feels even worse."

"Here." And with one swoop she whipped off her cloth sash, wrapped it around the stone, then stuffed it into my pocket. "Let's get going."

We tramped through the woods silently for a while. Finally, I broke the silence. "Sandi?"

"Huh?"

"Do you really think there is such a thing as . . . as that giant serpent Upshan?"

"Well, Sister Howling Wind certainly thinks so. And Nick buys the story."

"But what about you?"

Sandi stopped walking. "I don't know, Brook. Honestly I don't."

41

I turned to look at her. "That's my problem, too. One part of me says no way—it's got to be a myth. But then what about that tribe wiped out with no enemies and no clues?"

"Oh, there were clues all right. Real clues."

I raised one eyebrow. "I don't remember her telling of any clues."

Sandi broke off a twig, stripping it. "Usually she mentions them in later sessions—" Sandi paused abruptly and held her finger to her lips.

"What?" I whispered, drawing closer.

"Hear that?"

"What?"

"That crunching sound." Sandi was scanning the woods behind her.

I listened closely, but didn't hear anything. "No. I don't hear anything, just the birds—"

Then I heard it. A heavy crunch, followed by another coming from somewhere up the dry creek bed.

We both gasped.

"Run!" Sandi shouted, springing across the creek bed. "We're not far from our trailer. Move it!"

She didn't have to repeat herself. I was already close behind her, half running, half crawling, up the steep embankment that was still more than a mile from her home.

10

The faster we ran, the louder the crunch behind us. I arrived at the edge of a ravine. It was clogged with underbrush.

"Slide down!" Sandi called to me, breathless. "It's right behind us!"

I hit the ground, sliding under the bushes, slapping limbs from my face. "You back there?"

Sandi didn't answer.

I turned to scan the embankment. Then I saw her reach the edge. "I'm coming!"

I tried to claw my way back to where she was.

"No!" she screamed. "You don't have—"

Suddenly her foot caught on a protruding rock and she tumbled into me, rolling us down into the ravine.

When we stopped rolling, we were lying in a heap in a dry creek bed. Our shirts were torn in angles.

"Sandi?"

She lay there, not responding.

I crawled over. "Sandi, are you okay?"

She sat up, trying to shake her head. "Brook . . . what was that?" Her eyes were full of fear.

I sat back on my heels. "I don't know. Honest I don't. But we've got to get out of here."

She wobbled to her feet. "You said it. Let's go. Whatever was following us could come back."

"Can you make it?" I looked at Sandi's knee. There was a steady stream of blood.

"You bet," she struggled to say.

"Here, put your arm around my shoulders." I supported her waist as we hobbled toward the clearing. At last we could see the trailer. It was perched on a steep hillside. A bluetick hound lay at the door. He didn't bark. Just seeing him made me feel better, though.

We reached the door at last. Sandi leaned against a railing and fumbled for the keys. Suddenly the dog rose to its feet, howling furiously.

"Hurry!" Sandi urged. "It's still behind us."

Neither of us dared to look.

I shoved the door open, pulled Sandi inside, then slammed it shut. "There." Locking it quickly, I collapsed against the knob.

Sandi looked at her bloody knee. "I need to get this cleaned up."

I watched her as she headed for the bathroom. "Who, or *what*, could have been following us?"

"I don't know what's out there. And I'm sure not going back to find out," she said.

44

Just then a horn sounded out front.

"That must be Nick," Sandi said.

We both ran to the door, throwing it open wide. "Hurry up, Nick!" Sandi shouted. "Get inside, *quick!*"

He seemed to sense the danger immediately. Slamming the truck door, he ran like crazy toward the porch and entered the door just as the hound began barking and growling again toward the thicket.

11

"Boy, am I glad to see you." Sandi threw her arms around her husky brother.

"We," I corrected, telling him about our hike and the strange pursuer.

Sandi then told him about the loud crunching noise we heard and how we tumbled over each other into the ravine.

In an instant he reached into a closet and brought out a shotgun. I froze. The sight of any gun terrified me.

He strode toward the door, but Sandi stepped in the way. "No you're not. You're not stepping one foot out that door. I mean it."

Nick reached out to push her aside, then hesitated. "Don't do this to me, Sandi."

She folded her arms. "You heard me. Who knows what would happen if you went out there. I've already lost Mom. I couldn't bear to lose you, too."

At the word *Mom* his shoulders sagged a little. He reluctantly put the shotgun back.

I felt sorry for Sandi, but I didn't have time to dwell on it. She was already telling Nick about Brat's strange stone.

His hazel eyes widened in interest. "It sounds really unusual. Come on in here. I've got scads of books on rocks. Let's see if we can find out what it is."

We followed Nick through the narrow trailer to a small bedroom. The walls were lined with stacks of books and posters. In the corner was a computer surrounded by piles of papers. It looked more like a library workroom.

"See what I mean?" Sandi motioned to the books. "My brother the brain."

Nick ignored her. "Did you bring it?"

"Sure did." I worked it out of my jeans pocket.

He took it, unwrapping it briskly. One glance, though, and he let out a low whistle. For a moment he just stared at it, turning it slowly.

"Well?" I asked after what seemed an hour.

He looked up as though he just saw me for the first time. "Well what?"

"Well, can you look this up in your books?"

He looked down at the twinkling stone. "I don't need to. Not in any geology books, that is. They only deal with earthen rocks."

"So what are you saying?"

"Just that this is no earthen rock." He held it up, watching the scarlet and lavender fires. Then he looked at Sandi. "You know what this is, Sis. So why didn't you tell her?"

She glared at him. "No I don't. I've never seen a rock like this in my life."

"No, but you know what it is." He looked down at it again. "Or at least where it came from."

"Stop it!" She was almost screaming.

"I kept telling you the legend was true. So don't get mad at me now just because I'm holding proof in my hands."

"Hey!" I was getting scared. "Remember me? How about letting me in on this big discussion?"

Sandi sat down on the bed, flopping backward. "Go ahead, Nick. You're the one who keeps talking about the cursed mountain and all. Go ahead and tell Brook. But remember, Brook, this is just his research."

"And Sister Howling Wind," Nick added. "Not to mention—"

"Get on with it, Nick."

He then began to explain the legend of the giant serpent Upshan. Sandi insisted we had heard all that at the campfire session.

"Did she get to the part about Upshan's revenge?"

Sandi shook her head. I noticed I was shaking.

"Well, if anyone violates the *kontai*—that's Upshan's home—then he sends his Night-Twisters with the first of two warnings."

"Night-Twisters?" I ventured. I vaguely remem-

48

bered Sister Howling Wind mentioning that term in her story.

"Certain deadly snakes that carry out his commands."

Like rattlesnakes? I wanted to ask but didn't. "Hold it," I insisted. "Warnings? You mean, as in not to go near his home again?"

Nick smiled faintly. "I wish. No, once his *kontai* has been violated, there is no second chance. At least not that I know about. The warning is to let one know he—or she—has now become the target of a death stalk."

A trail of cold traveled up my spine. *Death stalk?* It sounded gruesome.

He leaned his arm on his computer. "Anyway, the Night-Twisters, according to legend, marked their victims. They did this by leaving a black stone with scarlet and lavender hues." He held the rock up to the light. "The exact colors that are in Upshan's feathers."

I stood there, trying to sort all this out. But every avenue led me back to the same conclusion—that stone was meant for us, Dad and me. But why? What had we ever done to this Upshan? We lived on Marrowbone Mountain, not on some *kontai* or whatever.

"Listen, you two, I've got to—" But my words were drowned out. The hound was again barking like crazy.

We ran to the living room about the time someone knocked on the door. Sandi waved us to be quiet as she tiptoed to the window. She took one look then turned around. All the color had drained from her face. "It's a state trooper," she said, her voice shaky.

"Hello," the trooper shouted. "Anyone in there?"

Nick opened the door.

The tall officer scanned Nick. "Are you Nick Ponder?"

"Yessir."

Sandi stepped out of the shadows. "I'm Sandi."

"You two better come with me. There's been an accident."

12

I had never ridden in a police car before. It was unnerving.

So was Sandi's crying. It only brought back that horrible incident we had just survived. What had been following us anyway?

I tried to console her as she sobbed on my shoulder. Nick was beginning to cry, too. If only the officer could tell them how badly their dad had been hurt. Instead, all he would say was that there had been an "accident." It was somewhere in the mountains, and Mr. Ponder had been taken to the village hospital.

Events were turning more gruesome with each passing minute.

Once we arrived, all three of us rushed to the information desk. I stood back as Sandi and Nick got the room number, but Sandi grabbed my hand.

"No," I insisted. "You two go ahead. I'll wait here. He'll want his family."

"Please?" Sandi pleaded. "I . . . I may need you."

I slipped my arm around her and said a silent prayer. "Let's go."

Once inside his room, we all breathed a sigh. At least there were no tubes, and his eyes were open. But his chest looked like it was in a plaster cast. And one leg was suspended by cords.

Both children fell on his neck, bringing a groggy smile to his face. I was glad they took their time loving him. It gave me time to dry my eyes.

In slow, thick speech, he began to explain he only had two cracked ribs and a broken ankle.

This brought a relieved expression to Sandi's and Nick's faces. Okay, to mine, too.

Then his long face grew serious. He looked up at Nick. "You were right, son."

"About what?"

Mr. Ponder then looked over at me. I was standing at the foot of his bed. Hesitating, he finally whispered, "I must have gotten too close, son. You were right all along."

Nick glanced over at Sandi and whispered, "See. There's still more proof."

Nick turned to say something to his dad, but he had drifted into sleep.

We tiptoed quietly from the room and walked back to the hospital lobby. I was dying to ask Nick what his father meant when he said he got too close. But Nick and Sandi became involved in business. They said they needed to contact their dad's out-of-state business partners. So I gave Sandi a hug and excused myself, saying I was going to meet Dad at the library before he left. Just as I reached the door, I turned.

"Here, Nick." I held out the mysterious stone. "You're into rocks. You can have this for your collection."

He stepped back, palms raised. "Thanks, but no thanks."

I looked at him. You would've thought I was offering a ticking bomb. "But you were so interested in it."

"I'm also interested in staying alive." He must have read my expression. "Sorry, Brook. But I've got Dad and Sandi to think about, too."

Stunned, I found my way out into the bright sunlight. But the sun didn't warm the chill that had settled over me. No question about it—Mr. Ponder's injury, this stone, and the legend of Upshan had to be linked.

But did that also include the "creature" that had followed Sandi and me?

My sleep that night was troubled by nightmares of rattlesnakes and monsters chasing me through the woods. I awoke with a jolt, my forehead perspiring and my heart thumping against my chest.

I lay awake in bed for what seemed like hours, until the sunlight crept in through the window. I got up and padded across the floor to the kitchen to start breakfast.

Over breakfast, I told Dad about Mr. Ponder's accident, though I was careful not to mention anything about Upshan's revenge and the strange stone.

"Was he hurt badly?" Dad asked.

"Not really. Just a couple of broken ribs and a broken ankle."

"Did he say how the accident happened?"

"No. At least I didn't hear his explanation."

"I'm sorry he had an accident. But I'm glad to know his injuries aren't critical."

After breakfast, Dad said he had to go to the library

for a while. As usual, he tried to talk me into going, too, but I told him I had plans for the day.

But no sooner was he gone than I started to get uptight. Nothing to do, no one to talk to—I wanted to scream.

So I called Mom. But she wasn't at home. This made me even more antsy. If I couldn't talk to Mom, then I had to face it. And thinking about Upshan's warning—if Nick was right—and the incident in the woods were things I didn't want to face. Not to mention the idea that the rattlesnake I saw in the dresser drawer could be one of Upshan's Night-Twisters.

Whenever I face a humongous problem, I crave fudge. It jump-starts my brain. I went to the kitchen and made a pan of fudge, then went to my room.

I sat in the middle of my bed, eating fudge and asking myself *why?* Why was this happening to me? What had I done to become the victim of Upshan's death stalking?

Suddenly I didn't want any more fudge. A headache was starting behind my eyebrows, and I just wanted to nap.

And I guess I did, because the next thing I knew I was aware I was on my stomach and something cold was pressing against my left arm. In fact, it felt cold and kind of wet, too. *Strange,* I thought, *Brat was never cold and clammy.*

Then my eyes flew open. *Oh, please . . . no!* I fought

the impulse to scream. "Brat?" I uttered in a small voice. "Brat?"

The coldness reacted to my voice. It seemed to quiver, then contract.

It's moving!

I sprang to a sitting position. There on my bed was a huge snake pulling into a tight coil. Its tongue flickered waves of warning.

"Help!" I screamed, jumping backward to the floor. *"Please, somebody!"* I stumbled out the door straight for the front porch. *"Please!"* I kept shouting. *"Please . . . Please . . . Please!"*

But my screams wouldn't drown out my thoughts—a real live snake had crawled into bed with me! I scraped my nails against my left arm until it began to ooze blood.

I hurried down the back road toward the village and the library. I knew Dad would be there, but I wasn't going there to see him. I needed to do some research—on Native American folklore, on the story of Upshan and the Night-Twisters.

I squinted through the library window. Dad was chatting with a man at the counter. I waited until he went back to the study room before I slipped in.

I asked for the section on Native American lore. The

woman at the desk looked at me. "Any tribe in particular?"

I leaned over the counter. "The Tocagons," I whispered.

"Oh, a local tribe, then." She took me to the back of the library, to a room labeled, NATIVE AMERICAN INFORMATION AND ARTIFACTS. Every wall held blankets and niches filled with pottery. In the center was a replica of a Native American dwelling. It resembled an igloo, but it was made out of terra-cotta.

On the wall was a poster of Sister Howling Wind. Under her stark picture was the announcement of her next story hour.

I got an idea. "You know, I got to hear her once." I motioned to the poster. "She's good."

"Indeed she is."

"But . . ." I hesitated.

The librarian looked up from the card catalog. "But what?"

"Well, I just wonder how much of what she says is true." I made a faint laugh. "You know, how much is just to entertain her audience."

The woman straightened her back. "You obviously don't know her very well."

I agreed, sorry that I had brought it up.

"Sister Howling Wind," the woman continued, "is a living history of her people. She never fabricates stories, never. The only time she dips into fiction is with the very young. You know, myths about the rabbit and the deer. Things like that."

I took a deep breath. "But what about that giant serpent? Upshan, is it?"

She riveted me with her gaze. "What about it?"

"I mean, about it killing her people and all." I faked a cough. "I mean, come on."

She shrugged. "Stranger things have happened." She then began to rattle off other lost tribes and people worldwide. She said they had all vanished mysteriously. "So who's to say she's wrong? After all, she lived before and after the incident. Who else is a better authority?"

Again I nodded. But this was not what I wanted to hear.

She finally left me at the Tocagon stack. I flipped through musty book after book. None seemed to mention Upshan by name. They only alluded to some "devastating disaster of unexplained origin." Yet they all admitted there was no evidence of an earthquake, invasion, or epidemic.

Then I saw it—a faded sketch on the back page. It was the most hideous creature I'd ever seen. Scrawled on the wall of a cave was a broad serpent with feathers bristled. Its mouth was open, its long fangs dripping venom. And its eyes were slits, casting a look of hate from their tiny pupils. They seemed to throb off the page.

I slammed the book shut.

Shelving the books quickly, I hurried outside, my pulse beating rapidly. Closing my eyes, I could still see that face, those fangs, those eyes. The cold, taunting stare still burned its image in my brain. And the size of the beast! It dwarfed a man sketched close to it.

I breathed deeply the mountain air, hoping it would revive my courage. I started walking toward home but stopped suddenly at a sporting goods store. A hammock, I decided, would be a safer bed from now on. I went in the store, located an inexpensive model, and made my purchase. When I went back outside, I heard a honk. Turning, I saw it was Nick. He was stopped at a red light.

"Hey, stranger," he called out of his truck. "Want a lift?"

I ran to his cab. "Is Sandi home?"

"Yes, but up to her elbows in work." He adjusted his mirror. "She's doing all Dad's insurance papers for the accident." He threw open the door. "Get in. I'm going by the back road."

I sat down and breathed deeply, putting my bag on the floor. As we drove beyond the tourist shops and motels, I looked at Nick. If I couldn't get to Sandi, he would have to do. "How's your dad?"

"Much better. He'll be out in a day or two."

"Great!" I counted slowly to ten. "Nick?"

"Hum?"

"What exactly happened to your father?"

"Oh, just a bad fall. You know how these mountains are."

"But back in his room he told you 'I got too close.'" I cleared my throat, then flicked something off my knee. "Too close to what?"

Nick shrugged as he turned off to the back road that led up the mountain. "I don't remember that. Of course, I was pretty upset that afternoon."

"But I remember. And he even told you that you were right." I turned and looked squarely at Nick. "What were you right about?"

He let out a whistle. "Man, Brook, you're worse than a lawyer. You know that?"

I smiled weakly. "Maybe Dad's rubbing off on me. Then you were trying to show him the stone, remember? What did that have to do with his getting too close?"

"Hey, speaking of your dad, I ran into him this morning. He was down at—"

"*Dad?* You saw Dad?" I froze. "What did you tell him?"

"About what? Ah, Brook, you mean you haven't shown him the lightning stone?"

I scrunched down on the hard seat. "No way. And don't you ever mention it, Nick Ponder. You've got to promise!" This cinched it—I was not going to tell Nick about my fanged sleep mate either.

There was silence. Only the crunch of gravel under the tires.

I sat up. "I mean it. You've got to promise you won't mention anything about Upshan or death stalking."

"Listen, Brook, you need to—"

"Promise, Nick. I mean it."

"Okay, okay, but only if you tell him everything . . . and soon."

"I will," I said under my breath, "provided you tell me one thing."

"Shoot."

"What have we done to be marked for death?"

15

Nick opened his mouth, hesitated, then said, "I can't. I just can't. Sorry, but I promised Sandi." He swerved around a gully. "So if you hear it, it'll have to come from her."

I folded my arms. At last I felt near my answer. "Good. Then forget my place. Drive me to yours."

But Sandi wasn't at the trailer. Only the bluetick hound. She left Nick a note saying she had walked to the village. She said she had to get their dad's signature on some papers.

"Just great," I groaned, flopping down on the couch. Just when I was going to get the information.

"Sorry." Nick then disappeared into his room. "There're some cold drinks in the refrigerator."

I thanked him but declined. I said I would go on home.

He came to his door. "I'll take you in just a minute. I'm trying to find something."

I headed toward the door with my bag under my arm. "That's okay. I can walk. It's just—"

"Brook, don't you get it?"

I held my hand on the doorknob. "You mean I shouldn't walk alone. Is that it?"

"Or at all, if I were you. And that goes for your dad, too. You saw what happened to you and Sandi the other day."

Boy, if he knew the whole truth!

"But I can't just wall myself up in the cabin."

"Here it is!" He practically ran out of his room. He was holding an old book with a stiff, faded binding. "I wanted you to read this for yourself."

I followed his finger to a paragraph. It was under the subtitle: DEATH STALKING OF THE ANCIENT UPSHAN.

The words made my hands tremble slightly. But I managed to read that once a "victim" has transgressed Upshan's cave, he or she receives two warnings, according to Tocagon legend.

"Two?" I said out loud before I caught myself.

Nick shut the book. "Exactly. So see? You've only received the death stone. The stalking doesn't really begin until after the second warning."

"Which is?" I reached for the book, but he held it back.

"I don't know. But the fact is you're not a target yet."

I stared at him. No question about it—he wasn't telling me all he knew. "Nick?"

"What?" He was busying himself with his books.

"Nick, look me straight in the eye and tell me you don't know the second warning."

"Ah, Brook. Chill out, okay?"

"Chill out? In case you haven't noticed, Dad and I are fast becoming targets of some . . . some giant monster." I couldn't believe I was uttering these words. "And why? What was our big crime?"

The phone rang, making us both jump. Nick grabbed for it, looking relieved that he was off my hook. "Oh, hi, Mr. Darrow. Yes, yes, she's right here."

I snatched the receiver. "Dad?"

"Brook, Hon. I'm glad I tracked you down."

I apologized for not telling him where I would be. But his voice sounded strange. "Are you okay?"

There was silence. "Brook, why would you do that to Brat?"

"Brat? Is there something wrong with him?"

"You mean you don't know?"

"Know what?" My eyes began to sting. "Dad, is Brat okay?"

16

Dad explained that he came home to find Brat cowering under the porch. Despite every effort, he wouldn't come out. "So I got on my hands and knees and crawled under there. That's when I saw it."

"Saw what?" My voice was trembling. *He's found a snake nest,* I thought.

"The—well—the tattoo, I guess."

"Tattoo?" I stiffened. "You mean someone tattooed my dog?"

"I guess it's a tattoo. I mean, it's there on his back. No fur left. Only an image of something like a snake, I guess. But it's got feathers, would you believe."

I gripped the receiver. "I can't believe what you're saying."

"And you didn't know about this?"

"Dad! Would I knowingly let somebody hurt my Brat?"

"No, of course not." His voice was low and apologetic. "I'm sorry, Brook. I don't know why I ever thought you would be a party to this."

But I really wasn't listening. I was too busy telling Nick to drive me home quickly. "Be there in a minute, Dad." And I hung up the receiver as Nick headed for the door.

"Your dog hurt?" he asked as we hopped in the truck.

"He better not be," I answered through a tightened jaw. "He just better not be."

In the jeep on the way to the veterinarian, I held Brat so tightly he squealed. "Sorry, boy." I ruffled his ear. Poor Brat. I still couldn't bear to look down at him in my lap. That ugly tattoo—or branding—glared up at me, taunting me. Who would do such a thing to a sweetheart like Brat?

Or *what*?

Dad assured me we were almost there. I was glad, because there could be an infection. We discovered the village had no veterinarian, so we had to drive down to the valley. The nearest big town was more than sixty miles away. I just hoped their vet had treated something like this before.

The veterinarian lived on a farm, and her small office was attached to a horse barn. She came to the door when we drove up the gravel road.

I hurried past her with Brat in my arms.

"Put him on the table over there." She motioned to a small examining table.

Dad told her we had found him with this odd tattoo on his back.

She didn't say anything as she probed it. But I watched her eyebrows rise slightly. She then took a smear of the bright scarlet color and put it on a slide. "Keep him calm," she instructed. She placed the slide under a microscope and began to study it.

Dad and I waited anxiously. I felt a lump forming in my throat. When she didn't say anything, I couldn't take it any longer.

"Is he going to be okay?"

She looked up, startled, as though she had forgotten I was there. "I don't see why not."

I let out a deep sigh, gathering Brat to me.

"But this is the strangest thing," she continued.

My heart thudded. "What?"

"This color the vandal used. It doesn't have any dye or stain pigmentation."

"What do you mean?"

"Just that its source is unknown. Every dye has pigments." She looked at it again. "I wonder where it came from," she said, more to herself than to us.

All of a sudden, I didn't want Dad to hear any more about it. So I thanked her, asked if the fur would ever grow back, and if Brat needed any medicine.

She shook her head at the idea of medication but said there was no answer to the fur question. "It just depends on how toxic this strange dye is."

I was already backing out the door as Dad wrote a

check. When I got to the car, I heard the veterinarian ask Dad to call her. She said she was curious about the color. "I want to know if his fur returns normally."

I had to swallow a nervous laugh. *Normal?* Was anything normal these days, for Dad, me, and now poor Brat? I scooped him up and snuggled him under my throat. "At least you're going to live, fella," I said, thanking God.

By the time we got home, I was exhausted. The whole day seemed to collapse on me, so I begged off on kitchen duty. Dad said he only wanted a sandwich anyway.

I knew I'd need his help to hang the hammock. After he ate, I explained that the old bed gave me the creeps (he didn't know I meant it literally!) and that I had decided a hammock would be more comfortable. I could see he was tired and he didn't object. We installed my new bed right away so we both could get some sleep.

After he left the room, I hopped in and lay there. *I've just got to see Sandi.* After the snake in my bed and Brat's attack, things were really getting out of hand. What's more, Dad was growing suspicious. On the ride home he kept talking about the strange color. "What kind of prankster would do such a thing?" He grew silent, then added, "I don't like any of this, Brook."

I didn't answer. I watched the countryside whiz by. Neither do I, I wanted to shout. But I couldn't draw him into this whirlwind, not now, at least. One victim at a time seemed to be Upshan's plan.

17

Waiting nervously, I sat in the dark. He promised he would be right over. Looking up, I could tell Dad's light was definitely out, so we would have time to talk. Now, if he would just show up.

Twenty minutes. Thirty minutes. I hugged my knees as some night birds overhead screeched at the moon. *Hurry*, my breathing kept saying, *hurry, hurry.*

"Brook?"

I jumped to my feet. "Nick?"

A streak of light cut over the ground. I ran toward the dark figure holding the light.

"Thanks for coming, Nick. I really mean it."

"No problem. But do we have to talk out here in the dark?"

"No, come in. Dad's asleep, so I'll turn my CD player on low. He's used to that, and we can talk by the fire."

We went inside. I adjusted my CD player to just the right volume. I offered Nick some corn chips.

"How did you know barbecue is my favorite?"

"Okay, I'll take the credit. But the truth is, it's mine, too."

He took a noisy bite. "What's this about some weird dye?"

I told him abut Brat's tattoo and how the vet had said the dye didn't show any pigmentation.

He shook his head. "Uh-uh. I don't buy that. All dyes, stains, and paints have pigmentation. No exception."

I now knew I had called the right person. "But not according to Brat's doctor."

"Look here, Brook." Nick leaned back on one elbow. "That is like saying human skin doesn't have pores."

I shrugged. "Still, I'm wondering, since the image was a feathered serpent."

"Oh, no," Nick groaned, rolling onto his back. "Don't try that again. You know what I said: Ask Sandi."

"But Sandi doesn't have your background. She doesn't know about fiery stones and dyes without pigments."

"Oh, yeah? Doesn't know or won't tell?"

Bingo! I thought. That was the reason I wanted to talk to Nick again. Sandi was too concerned with my feelings to level with me while Nick was so interested in the unusual he might just slip up once. "Then you won't even look at my dog's back?"

He got to his knees. His expression was pleading.

"Look, if I do, the next thing you'll do is take my opinion as fact."

"No, I won't. I promise. I just respect your knowledge. Besides, you know more about these mountains than most experts."

"Says my crazy sister."

"Says your smart sister," I corrected.

"Brook?"

Nick and I froze. It was Dad's voice.

"Come on." I hurried Nick out to the kitchen, aiming him at the back door.

"Okay, I'm going." But Nick stopped at the door. For a minute he looked like he was about to say something, but thought better of it. "I still say you need to talk to Sandi. I'll go with whatever she says."

"That's what I'm afraid of," I told him. "I want the truth, not some story to make me feel better."

He turned to leave. "Well, this much I can tell you: The legend of Upshan and the Night-Twisters is too serious for anyone to play around with. Did Sandi tell you about that souvenir shop in the village?"

I nodded as my throat tightened.

"Well, my word of advice is to stay close to home, never stay alone for very long, and get out of here the minute your dad is finished."

I watched as Nick disappeared into the dark woods. In a way, I felt worse than I did when I called him. He knew volumes more than he was telling.

73

"Brook? Is someone down there? I thought I heard voices." Dad's voice was heavy with sleep.

"Sorry, Dad. I'll turn off the CD player and go to bed."

"Good night," he called in a drowsy voice.

I wish, I thought glumly. *Just one good* anything *would be a definite change.*

18

I thought I heard a phone, but it sounded distant, almost swimmy. Somehow it mingled with my dreams. Then my eyes flew open.

Breakfast! Sunlight filled the room and I knew Dad needed to get to the library. Throwing my legs over the side of the bed, I jumped to my feet and grabbed my robe.

But just as I got to my door, I heard Dad say, "No, Sandi, here's Brook now. Hold on, okay?" He offered me the receiver.

"Hey there." Sandi's voice sounded irritatingly chipper for 7:00 A.M. "Listen, it's obviously too early for you to talk, so go scramble those eggs. I'll call back later."

"No!" Then I caught myself. I couldn't sound too urgent in front of Dad. "I mean, no, let me call you, okay?" I wasn't about to let her slip away again. "Is around eight o'clock okay?"

"Fine. But, Brook?"

"Yes?"

"Are you okay? I mean your voice sounds kind of strange."

I peered around to see where Dad was. "Listen, Sandi, I've got heaps to tell you. You won't believe what's been going on over here."

She then suggested that she drop by instead.

"Nick doesn't want you to."

"What do you mean?"

"Your brother says it's not safe to walk over here."

"That's just it—he's going to drop me by on his way into the village."

The next hour dragged like an hour of math class. I thought Dad would never find a book he'd misplaced. Then Mom called to tell us the sink had backed up but the plumber had fixed it. By the time he was finally out the door, I was a basket case. I could just see Dad deciding to study at the cabin today, ruining everything.

By the time Sandi arrived, I was so revved I practically dragged her off the porch.

"Wow!" She laughed, sitting down on the sofa arm. "You sure do snap out of being a sleep-zombie fast." She leaned over absentmindedly to pet Brat. "Hey there, boy." Then she stopped. "Brook, what's wrong with Brat's back?"

I then told her everything, both about the snake and Brat's "tattoo." She sat there, her expression wide-eyed.

"So you've just got to help me."

"I don't get it. How can I help?"

"By telling me everything—*everything*—you know about this Upshan and his warnings. Are these snake prowlers part of the . . . the death stalk?"

She slid down to the sofa. "Ah, Brook, I'm the wrong person to ask. You—"

"No you're not, Sandi Ponder. You're the only person."

"But Nick knows all that stuff. Not me."

I sat down beside her. "But I tried him. He absolutely will not tell me anything more. He says it has to come from you."

"I don't know why." She was shaking her head slowly. "I'm not sure I even buy that stuff anyway."

"Buy it or not, I need to know." I turned to face her fully. "Could this attack on Brat be the second warning?"

Sandi stood up. She was fidgeting with her belt buckle. "Don't do this, Brook. I mean it. You and your Dad aren't going to be here long. I'm sure you'll be okay." She touched my arm. "Really."

I pulled away. "I can't believe you won't help me." I held my voice steady though I was shaking. "I thought we were friends."

"We are, Brook, don't you see? That's why I can't let you torment yourself like this. You're being drawn into something no one can prove."

"And I guess things like the hidden rattlesnakes, the lightning stone, something following us in the woods, and Brat's tattoo with eerie dye are just coincidences."

She drew a deep breath. "Just play it cool, okay? Stay close in, keep doors and windows shut, and Brat inside—I bet you'll be just fine."

I couldn't believe this was the same Sandi who had been so concerned day after day. Then it hit me. I stood up, my back straight. "I'll tell you who's playing it cool, Sandi Ponder." I felt my anger rise. "You are. You and your brother. You're just afraid to help me because he . . . it might start stalking your family, too."

She didn't answer. She just turned and walked out the door.

I stood there, angry, and yet sorry I had lost my cool. Why should I be angry at Sandi for protecting her family? How would I know what it's like to lose a mother?

I crumpled down on the sofa. Brat jumped into my lap, and the sight of his back made me feel even more wretched. As I scratched his ears, I knew I now had to see this through on my own. Sandi was too afraid to get involved, and I had no right to blame her. I reacted first and thought second.

Sandi? It just dawned on me she was now out there in the woods, alone. I jumped up, ran to the door, and called her name.

But there was no sign of my former friend anywhere.

"Sandi?" I kept calling. She couldn't be that far ahead. I kept running. How could she disappear so fast? "Sandi, answer me."

I followed our usual path toward the ravine. Overhead, the clouds were beginning to thicken, but I still had plenty of daylight left. "If you're making a game out of this, I'm—"

Suddenly I heard something to my right. It wasn't exactly a crunch or a snap, but it was definitely something. The sound came from beyond underbrush so dense it looked matted and tangled. "Okay, girl, you've had it now." And I began to tear my way through the green mass. "I'm serious, Sandi. Come on out. My hands are already bleed—"

Swoosh! Suddenly I felt the ground give way under my feet as I fell into darkness. Tumbling and twisting, I knocked against rough, slimy rocks, finally landing in squishy mud.

For a moment I just sat there, dazed. *What kind of hole is this?* I tried to focus on my prison with the tiny light I'd opened in my fall. But nothing, only the smell of darkness.

I checked my arms, then my legs. Nothing seemed broken. But I felt a sting on my side. I touched it and flinched. My fingers felt wet, so I knew I was bleeding. But how badly?

I pushed myself to my feet. "Ouch!" My side was really throbbing now, but I was more concerned with getting out of there. After all, no one knew I was out in this mountain wilderness to start with. And in this dense underbrush?

Running my hands frantically along the wall, I felt damp, mossy stones. *This must have been an old well,* I thought. *Or a mine shaft,* I decided as I felt for loose stones. Dad did say this mountain range was full of caves, so maybe there were mines, too.

Hey, what's this? I felt a stake jutting out from the dark wall. Maybe the miners placed these all the way up as a type of ladder. I began to grope for another stake—yes!—then another. But there was a hole where one had been.

Then I sensed something moving around me. Something cold and clammy brushed against my sandaled foot.

I shrank against the wall. *Rattlesnakes!* my brain screamed. But how many? I doubled up in a rigid ball. My side was now screaming with pain, but I didn't care—I was trapped in some snake pit too dark to even see my enemies.

At first my mind short-circuited. I could pull nothing up on the screen, only panic. Then my whole body began to tingle, recalling the clammy touch of that snake against my foot.

I slid down the wall, slowly, slowly, remembering from somewhere that snakes strike at any abrupt motion. So I sat there, huddled in a ball, listening to the agitated rattling out there in the dark somewhere.

You can't sit here forever, an annoyed voice said in my mind. *You've got to make a move. No one knows to look for you out here.*

But I refused to budge. No way was I going to cause some rattlesnake to sink his deadly fangs into me.

I tried to remember what snakes ate. Mice? Yes, I remembered a boy at school feeding his pet green snake live mice. *Yuck!* But what about these big rattlesnakes?

Rats! I bet they live on rats! I strained again to see in the dark hole. *Am I trapped down here with snakes and rats, too?*

The thought made me clasp my arms tighter around my knees.

Hey, wait a minute! Didn't I read somewhere that snakes have poor hearing? If that's so, then maybe I can hold on until they start searching for me. They will search, won't they? Then I could at least yell out my location.

But my thought was interrupted. Something in

front of me moved. I couldn't see it. I couldn't feel it. But I sensed that it moved.

I tried to swallow, but my throat was too dry. I buried my face on my knees. *Don't move!* I ordered my reflexes. *Don't move! One's close!*

Then I felt it. A cold, wet creature began to slide over my open toes. Slowly . . . slowly. It was all I could do not to sling my sandaled foot free. Slowly the clammy underbelly slithered over the flesh of my foot. I bit my lip so hard that I tasted salt. Then after what seemed like days, the long reptile finally crossed over my foot, leaving me limp and tremulous.

At first I wanted to shout for joy. I had not been fanged by this huge deadly serpent!

But the realization that I might become a "rug" for the other venomous snakes down here cleared my mind really fast. *Bitten or not, I've got to get out of here. I can't go through that again, ever.*

And stay sane.

But just as I was about to slide slowly up the wall to a standing position, I thought I heard someone say "Sandi." *Wishful dreaming*, I decided as I continued to edge my way up, inch by inch.

"Sandi? Where are you?"

My heart thudded. "Nick?" I shouted, forgetting the snakes. "Nick, I'm down here!"

"Who called my name?" His voice sounded not too distant overhead.

"It's me. Brook. I'm in some well. There are snakes. Help, *please!*"

Then I strained to hear. Nothing.

Now the snakes were moving. I didn't dare risk another word, and my spirits hit bottom. *He didn't hear me.*

Just as I was going to feel the wall for more stakes, I heard the rustle of bushes overhead.

"Nick? I'm down—" A huge shaft of light hit my face. Squinting, I could see his outline.

"Brook? What're you doing down—don't move!" His voice was emphatic. *"D-o-n'-t m-o-v-e!"* I'll be right back."

When he got back he had what looked like an old rope. "This'll work just fine," he assured me. "The other end's tied to a tree."

I didn't care what it was tied to. I was already reaching for the makeshift ladder. Getting farther and farther away from this snake pit was all that mattered.

But just as I lifted my left foot off the muddy bottom, I felt a thud on my heel. I shook it but it still felt heavy.

"Nick, something's wrong with my foot." I tried to twist around to see what made my sandal so heavy.

He leaned over the opening above. I thought he made a muffled sound, but instead, he kept urging me to hurry. "You'll be okay. Just keep climbing."

I did. But something about my left heel felt heavy.

When I was halfway up, he reached for me. I clasped firmly onto his wrists then rappelled against the wall until I could belly over the opening.

"There!" he said at last, as I sprawled facedown on the forest floor. Too exhausted to breathe, I still reached back for my left sandal.

"No!" Nick yelled. And with that he yanked it off my foot.

"Hey!" I complained, rolling on my back. "That—" But I sucked in my breath.

Dangling from the heel of my sandal was the longest snake I had ever seen. His fangs were still embedded in the rubber heel, making him a victim of his own attack. His long body was twisting and floundering angrily.

My whole body spasmed as I squeezed my eyes shut. I was just one thin sandal away from dying in some hidden snake pit.

Two days after the snake pit incident, I was still trying to get my nerves under control—while trying to convince Dad everything was cool. I needed an outing. So I was glad we were low on groceries. This gave me an excuse to ride to the village.

Once I was in the store, I got the idea that a cookout that night would be a great treat for Dad. For me, too. Dad would prefer grilled chicken to hamburgers, and

I would make a big salad to go with it. I went to the produce section first.

Just as I was weighing the tomatoes, I felt a nudge in my side, right where I'd been scraped in my fall into the snake pit.

"Hi, Brook." The voice was low, hesitant.

I swung around. There stood Sandi. She looked ill at ease, a loaf of bread in her hand.

"Want me to hold the scales steady?"

"Oh, Sandi." Tears welled in my eyes. I couldn't help it. "I'm so glad to see you."

Her expression brightened. "You are?" She squeezed my wrist. "Oh, Brook. I just hate what happened the other day. I haven't slept well in two nights. Nick either. He told me everything."

I fumbled for a tissue in my jeans pocket. "I'm sorry, but that . . . that snake pit's made me a basket case."

Sandi glanced around at a woman who was standing behind us. Her hands were full of turnips, and she was eyeing the scales. "Look. Let's go somewhere for a cold drink. I shouldn't have brought it up."

I didn't even answer. I quickly grabbed the tomatoes and practically threw them back on the pile.

Down the street we found an outdoor vendor selling hot dogs. We each bought one, piled on the relish, then sat on the long steps to the ski lift. The sun was bright, but there was still a nip in the air.

"Listen, Brook," Sandi began, after swallowing a big bite.

"No, you listen. I can't tell you how sorry I am for what I said. I mean, I had no reason to blow up like that." I sneaked a glance at her.

She shrugged. "And why not? You were telling the truth."

"How's that?"

"Just that you were telling the truth," she repeated. "Nick and I were copping out on you about the warnings of Upshan. You told the truth when you said we were just protecting ourselves."

I rested my hot dog on my knee. "But why not? You had every right to protect yourself. I was wrong to get so angry."

"But I was wrong to not tell the truth. Mom wouldn't have approved. Telling the truth was always a big deal with her." Her voice grew thin and distant. I thought I saw a wisp of sadness in her expression. "So Nick and I made a decision. That ghastly snake pit finally opened our eyes."

I didn't say a word. My heart lunged in my ribs.

"We're going to come clean with you. The mystery of Upshan, the warnings, everything we know. Whether I believe it or not."

I grabbed her hand. "Oh, Sandi, thanks. I mean it. Thanks."

"But I want Nick in on this, too. And since Dad's still at the clinic, Nick won't be free until tomorrow morning." She took her last bite, then dusted her hands. "So can you drop over around nine or ten tomorrow?"

"You got it!" It felt so good to clear the air between us.

That afternoon I kept busy. I cleaned the rusty grill we found in the loft. Then I made the salad and skinned the chicken. I even made some pickle slaw the way Dad liked it. Everything was ready, but I couldn't get the fire started.

Then it started, but died out. After the umpteenth time, the fire started and kept burning. By the time the chicken was done, Dad was over two hours late.

I called the library. A recording said the closing hour was five P.M. "But it's already after seven," I told Brat.

I looked at my now charred "treat" for Dad. A finger of chill crept over my body. Outside it was getting dark, and Dad was never late without first calling. It was a big thing with him.

I went to the window and scanned the tiny road below. Nothing but shadows.

I went back to the kitchen and set the charred chicken on the counter. I wasn't hungry anymore.

By ten o'clock I was really frantic. This was not like Dad to be so late. I walked to my bedroom and flopped into my hammock. I closed my eyes and said a silent prayer, trying to force the negative images from my mind.

Sometime in the night I dozed off. I was startled awake by Brat's barking. "Dad?" I called out in the darkness. "Dad, is that you?"

No answer. But the barking grew louder.

My body went rigid with fear. *Brat would never bark at Dad.*

21

My hands were trembling as I rolled out of the hammock. I fumbled toward the door, then stopped. No way was I going out there unprotected. I felt around for anything I could use as a weapon. But there was nothing. I summoned all the courage I could and silently crept toward the front room.

I could see the reflected light from the fireplace. Brat sounded like he was under the kitchen table. That was odd. He usually barks at the door.

But one look at our living room and I could see why. It looked like a tornado had swept through. The sofa was knocked over, the lamp crushed, Dad's papers were scattered across the floor.

The window, which I had closed earlier, was wide open. I inched my way over to it. I stepped on something. Looking down I saw it was the lightning stone. The hewn rock, which I had hidden, was lying on the floor. *Who did this?* I wondered. *Who could know my hiding place?*

Reaching the window, I peeked outside. In the

moonlight I saw the outline of a huge mass. It was cylinder-shaped, dark and elongated.

I shrank back. *Upshan? Could it have been Upshan in here?*

I ran back to find Brat. But I stopped at the sight of something glittery near the front door. I leaned over to study it. It was a huge feather with iridescent hues of lavender and scarlet.

I kicked it under a cabinet. *Yuck!* An odd odor encircled me. It was sort of musty, yet biting, like the smell in old attics or . . . or walls and caves.

"Come on, boy," I commanded. He was still cowering under the table. He acted as scared as I felt. "Come in my room. It's okay." I tried to sound confident.

Together, Brat and I huddled in the dark. In the middle of my hammock I rocked us both. I began to pray harder than I ever had in my life.

I was so intent on my prayers I didn't hear the lock. But suddenly I heard someone yell, "Brook!"

"Dad?" I jumped out of the hammock, stepping on Brat's tail. "Dad, is it you?"

"Brook?" Then he paused. After a few seconds, he called my name again. This time there was irritation in his voice.

"Oh, Dad!" I ran over and threw my arms around him. "I'm so glad you're home." I willed myself not to cry. "You'll never believe what happened!"

He gave me a weak hug, then stepped back. Slowly

he surveyed the room. "I just don't believe this. Brook, you've never been this kind of girl."

I stared at him. "What do you mean?"

"This." He made a sweeping gesture to indicate the disheveled room. "Is this the influence of your new friends? A wild party when your dad's away?"

I kept staring at him. Is that what he thought? Suddenly I lost strength in my knees. Leaning against the wall I fought the stinging behind my eyes. "Dad, you know me better than that! How can you even think I would do such a thing?"

He ran his hand over his bald spot. "I know, Brook, I know. But here's the evidence."

I told him I woke up to find the room like this.

"You mean Nick didn't bring Sandi over with him?"

"Why would he do that?"

"When he delivered my message."

I held up my hand. "Wait a minute—what message?"

He explained he had to go to a man's house for a book, so he asked Nick to drive by to tell me he would be late. He said he saw Nick in the parking lot, and Nick had assured him he would deliver the message.

"But why didn't you just call?"

"The man doesn't have a phone. I didn't want to embarrass him by using a public phone."

I slumped against the wall. So that's why he was late. But why didn't Nick deliver the message? Then it occurred to me something may have come up. Sandi and Nick had a lot to do while their dad was recuperating.

Dad began to apologize for jumping to conclusions, wrong conclusions. But I wouldn't let him finish.

I watched as Dad surveyed the mess. Now I was worried he might suspect the truth.

He looked up. "This is frightening, Brook. To think I left you up here alone while . . . while . . ."

"Ah, it's okay. I always keep my door shut, and Brat's a terrific barker."

"Yes, but if it's some scavenger bear, poor Brat's no protection."

I went over to him and slid my arm around his waist. "He is with that killer bark. Why, he's so loud I bet that poor bear's halfway to the interstate."

Dad started to straighten the furniture but I stopped him. "Let's get some sleep first. We can clean up tomorrow."

He agreed reluctantly. But he insisted on sleeping in front of the fireplace. He said he had made enough bad decisions about me for one night.

"But now we are together and safe," I assured him.

I just wished I could believe the words I was saying.

The next morning, I got up over an hour before Dad woke up. I had to. This way I got the lightning stone hidden again safely. I put it behind another loose stone in the fireplace. And, more important, I had a chance to wrap the long, mysterious feather and tuck it under the sink.

By the time I called him to breakfast, he answered me from the front yard. "Come out here a minute, Brook."

I went to the porch. Dad was down by the bushes inspecting something.

"Can you believe this?" He pointed to a flattened path that led into the bushes. "Could a bear have done this?"

I didn't answer. My mouth was too dry to speak. But I would have gladly settled for a bear.

22

When we finally had breakfast, Dad dropped the bomb-shell. He said he was going to look for somebody to stay with me.

"Dad!" I scooted back from the table.

"I know, I know. But I can't leave you up here alone. You saw what could happen."

My mind raced. "But I won't be alone."

"You mean you'll come to the library with me?"

"No! I . . . I mean I'll talk to Sandi. We can work something out. And I always have the phone."

He sipped his coffee. He didn't seem convinced.

"I promise. Just let me check, okay?"

He put down his cup. "Well, okay. The two of you together ought to be all right."

By the time we finished our devotional, he looked more at ease. The intruder last night had really rattled him. *If he only knew,* I mused, then intentionally broke the thought. I didn't ever want to think about it either.

"Dad?" Sandi's voice sounded anxious when she answered the phone.

"Oh, sorry, Sandi, I'll let you go. I didn't know you were expecting—"

"No, no." Her voice was insistent. "It's just that he usually calls before now." She asked me what was up.

I told her everything about last night. She didn't say a word, but I sensed her listening intently. When I finally finished recapping the events, she remained silent.

"And another thing," I continued. "Dad asked Nick to give me his message. Do you know why he didn't?"

"My fault. Dad called and asked Nick to come by the hospital. Anyway, he told me to call you, but your line was busy." She paused. "Around eleven or so, I think."

I told her the phone was knocked on the floor, along with the other debris.

"Listen, Brook. You and I both know that was no bear, don't we?"

I agreed.

"And now there's this mysterious feather. Long as your arm, you say?"

"Longer, in fact."

"So we've got to get you to the only one who can help . . . and quick."

I was confused. "I don't get it."

"You will. Believe me, you will."

23

Nick's truck seemed to find every bump in the road. But I didn't care. The truth behind this mystery lay at the end of this steep mountain road. At least that's what Sandi promised. So I could be bumped through the roof and still not care.

"There it is!" Sandi pointed to a low house. It appeared to jut out from the hillside behind it. Hanging from every tree were drying skins and hides of animals. On the porch were many pots of ferns and herbs. A three-legged dog sprawled out on the top step.

Somehow it matched my vision of Sister Howling Wind's home. "You are coming in with me, aren't you?"

"Sandi is," Nick answered.

I started to protest, but he said she was as "up" on the legend as he was.

"Right, Sandi?" He pressed her to agree.

"Yeah, right . . . right." She seemed mad at him all morning.

As soon as we parked, the hound started barking. A tall, broad-shouldered man darkened the doorway.

"He doesn't look too friendly," I whispered as we picked our way to the porch.

"That's Fleet Hawk. He's one of her five sons." She waved to him, but he didn't move. "Don't worry. They're all cautious."

At the door he stepped aside. No words were exchanged. Inside the dark room I saw no furniture, only woven pallets dotting the floor. In the corner was a woodstove.

"Is Sister Howling Wind here?" Sandi spoke to Fleet Hawk like an old friend.

He didn't have time to answer. The old Tocagon sage appeared through a beaded doorway. She looked more curious than hostile. "You want me?"

"Yes," I spoke up. "I, uh, I would like to talk to you about something very urgent. At least to me and my dad."

She stood very still. Her sunken eyes didn't blink.

"You see, it's—" I hesitated. I suddenly felt her son's presence very keenly.

Somehow she must have sensed my uneasiness, because she said something in her tribal language. He nodded once, then strode out the door. I could hear Nick's truck growing distant on the gravel, and I felt a sinking in the pit of my stomach. All of a sudden I felt like Sandi and I were deserted in some tribal camp.

She asked us to sit on one of the pallets. She then

handed each of us a small bowl. In it she poured something like a cloudy green tea. I watched as she sat down across from us, sipping the drink. "Good for the stomach," she announced matter-of-factly.

I didn't wait for Sandi. I held my breath and took a sip. It was the least I could do to repay her for hearing me.

Hey, I thought, tasting the bitter brew, *this stuff tastes pretty good.* I began to tell her about the day Dad and I arrived, the strange carving, the dust image, and the rattlesnake.

She interrupted. "Where is your dwelling?"

"On Marrowbone Mountain," Sandi piped up.

The old woman nodded like she understood.

I then told her about the serpent Upshan. "I know it sounds crazy, but I think there may be a connection."

She sat there. "You have a right."

"I do?"

"But I do not tread on Upshan's terrain often."

I looked at Sandi. "She means," she murmured, "she doesn't like to talk about it."

"But your dwelling earns you the right, young one."

"I don't understand."

"When you live on someone's land, you have a right to know that person." She looked at me boldly. "That person's good spirit and bad."

I shook my head. "I'm sorry, Sister Howling Wind, but I'm still not with you. You speak of living on someone's land? Well, we live on—"

"The cursed *kontai*," she supplied.

"No! You said that's where Upshan lived. Our mountain is called Marrowbone."

"Yes, in English, young one. Because *kontai* in our language means 'the hollow of bone.'"

I looked at Sandi.

She looked crushed. "I'm sorry, Brook. But you had to know."

Sister Howling Wind continued to explain the serpent's home was located at the summit of our mountain. "It's in a cave, up on a bluff. It overlooks the river."

I couldn't believe we had been hiking just below this monster's lair. Now I needed to get more to the nitty-gritty. "You once mentioned feathers around its throat."

"Special feathers. Very special. You see, Upshan is very jealous of his home. If someone encroaches, that person is marked for"—she eyed me—"for death. He spares no one so bold."

"But what does that have to do with the feathers?" I felt Sandi slide her hand over mine.

"There are two warnings Upshan—or his servants, the Night-Twisters—leaves. One is a strange stone that captures his colors." She stopped to sip her tea. "Another is a feather from his own throat."

I turned my hand to grasp Sandi's. "You say the feather is the last warning?"

She nodded deeply. "The last before the actual attack."

I tried to breathe slowly to slow my pounding pulse. But my thoughts were swirling.

"Why, young one?" she asked. "Why do you appear so pale? Is it the drink? It can be too strong for some."

I steadied my voice. "I . . . I've got to tell you something, Sister."

24

Sister Howling Wind walked over to the stove. She stoked the fire in its belly. Then quietly she stirred something on the stove. The whole room filled with the aroma of herbs.

"You okay?" Sandi whispered.

I assured her I was, though my trembling showed otherwise.

When Sister Howling Wind took her seat again, I had decided how I would approach this subject. "These warnings—is there any way a marked person can reverse this death stalking?"

Her eyebrows rose. "Upshan is a strong force. Very strong."

"Then you're saying there's no escape?"

"Only that one must meet the mighty Upshan on his own ground."

I sat forward. "I don't understand."

"Well, the punishment falls because one draws too close to his cave. So to stop the death stalk, one must return Upshan's stone."

"You mean go into his cave?"

"More. To the ledge beyond the River of Tears. It flows in the bowels of his cave."

I felt like I'd just been punched in the stomach. Sitting there with Sandi's hand in mine, I felt completely off center.

But Sister continued to say no one had ever received his stalking in her lifetime. "No one but the son of our chieftain, that is."

I knew she was trying to comfort me, but it wasn't working. That brave and all of the Tocagons were wiped out as a result of his marking. And now I had received the same warnings.

I got to my feet, thanking her.

Sandi stared at me quizzically. But she also rose.

"Was there something you wanted to tell me?"

"No," I assured the old woman. "No, I have everything I need to know."

She looked down into her bowl. "So be it."

Once out on the porch, Sandi began to bombard me with questions. She couldn't believe I wasn't going to tell the Indian woman about my two warnings.

Instead, I suggested we walk down the road. Nick was due in fifteen minutes. "I need some fresh air."

She quickly agreed. As we stumbled down the deep gully, I told her I had made my decision: I would take the stone to Upshan's ledge.

She came to an abrupt stop. "You're kidding!"

I assured her I wasn't. What's more, it would be

done that afternoon while I was still free of Dad's protection. "Besides, I have his life to think about as well."

Sandi sat down on a rock. "Brook, I don't know. I mean—"

"Don't worry about me, Sandi. I'll be okay."

"But you don't have any protection, no weapons, not even a flashlight."

"Not the visible kind, if that's what you mean."

Sandi suddenly poked me, nodding to my left. There stood Fleet Hawk, Sister Howling Wind's son. He stood on the other side of a gully, motioning to us.

Sandi pointed to herself. "Me?"

He shook his head briskly, gesturing to me.

"He wants to see you," Sandi whispered from the corner of her mouth.

I swallowed hard. "What's this all about?" I hoped he didn't hear my question.

Sandi's expression was blank but there was a flicker of fear in her widened eyes.

"Oh, well." I got a running start and jumped the gully. "Tell Nick to wait if he gets here soon."

I walked over to Fleet Hawk, feeling a little nervous. I looked up into his broad face. "You wanted to see me?"

He didn't answer. He just motioned up to a cottonwood grove. I followed as he walked toward it with long strides. Once we got to the grove, he turned. "I heard everything."

"You did?"

He nodded slightly.

"You mean back at your mother's house?"

"You are going to the *kontai*."

I took a step backward. "How did you know? I just decided that a minute ago."

"I know. That is enough," he said simply.

"Is that wrong? I mean, is that . . . bad?"

He said nothing. Then he said, "It is like the wind."

I looked at him, puzzled. "The wind?"

"For mountain fires, it is bad." He motioned to the steep mountainside behind him. "But for trees, it scatters their seeds."

"So you're saying it all depends."

His dark eyes softened.

"But depends on what, Fleet Hawk?" I felt I was finally with someone who would tell me the truth.

"On your enemy."

I sighed. "I guess you mean its power. Well, Upshan sure seems like a megaenemy to me."

He reached up and grasped a limb. "Are you sure Upshan is your enemy?"

I tilted my head. "What do you mean?"

He shrugged.

"What are you trying to say?"

"Some enemies thrive in the open. Some lurk in the bushes. And how quickly the hunted identifies his enemy's location reveals who will conquer."

I shook my head. "I'm sorry, Fleet Hawk. I don't get it."

"Just remember how our braves of old used to set up camp at night. All would circle the fire, facing out toward the darkness."

"Oh, I see. You're saying I need to keep my back covered at all times."

He didn't nod but his eyes crinkled at the edges.

"You mean from the Night-Twisters." I shuddered. "Believe me, I've had enough contact with rattlesnakes for two lifetimes." I looked back to see if Nick had driven up yet. Sandi was still standing alone, trying to look cool, but I knew she was dying to know what Fleet Hawk and I were talking about.

Fleet Hawk turned to leave. Then he paused. "Remember, young one, these mountains are home to many kinds of snakes." He hesitated, then added, "Not just snakes that rattle . . . or crawl on their bellies."

I watched as he disappeared into the undergrowth. What did he mean by that? He was obviously trying to help me, but what help were riddles? Jumping back over the gully, I was glad to join Sandi again. She might be stubborn, but at least she didn't mask the truth.

She was full of questions, of course, but for some reason I didn't feel like telling anyone what Fleet Hawk had said. I felt too privileged that he had tried to help me.

"Okay, be that way," Sandi snapped in mock anger.

"Just because Fleet Hawk never talks to anybody makes your head swell."

"Really? Wow, I'm—" But I didn't have time to finish. The sound of spraying gravel meant Nick was coming.

Grabbing his door before he even stopped, she quickly told him everything. When she finally got to my decision to go to Upshan's cave that same afternoon, Nick let out a whoop.

"Way to go there, Brook!" He slapped the steering wheel as we climbed in. "You've got what it takes, girl!"

Sandi looked at her brother as if he had just landed from Mars. "What're you saying? Are you trying to get her killed?"

"Nope. It's just that I've been dying to catch a glimpse myself. So care if I go along?"

Sandi grabbed his arm, then released it. "Well, if you two are brave enough to face this thing, then so am I."

"Brook, I'll drive you by your cabin so you can get the stone."

"No need." I patted a pocket of my jeans. "I thought I might show it to Sister Howling Wind."

I looked at Sandi. "You don't have to come."

"And be the only one left behind? No, thanks." She cut a glance in my direction. "Besides, I'd have too much explaining to do if you and Nick were reported missing."

The words hung in the air like smoke. *Missing.* No

one spoke again as the truck groaned and jostled its
way higher and higher up the *kontai*.

25

A few hundred feet below the cave we had to abandon the truck. The path played out, and the cliff ahead was mostly brush and rock. Nick handed me a flashlight and gave Sandi a gallon jug filled with water. "In case we decide to spend the night," he quipped, grabbing three picks out of his flatbed.

"Ha . . . ha," Sandi responded flatly as she eyed the narrow climb ahead.

I personally was glad for some humor. It had been deathly quiet on the ride up. I tried to look steady, but I felt like a lump of Jell-O inside.

"This is the best time to go," Nick volunteered. He added that a snake's nature is to roam in the late day.

Memories of those snakes in the pit slithered into my thoughts. I could still feel that cold underbelly crawling over my bare foot and the thud on my heel when the angry snake struck for my flesh.

I tried to shake those thoughts away. But one thought would not vanish—those reptiles in the snake pit and in our cabin were vicious, but normal size. *But what about this monster Upshan?*

Together, we climbed up the ledge in front of the cave. At first I was almost glad the entrance was a little smaller than I imagined. But then I thought about being trapped in a tight spot with a giant snake. *The opening couldn't be too big*, I quickly decided.

We stood in front of the cave, catching our breath from the climb. But we couldn't take our eyes off the half-hidden entrance.

My skin began to crawl. "Well," I whispered, "here goes everything." I bent down and forced myself to creep into the darkness. Immediately I was engulfed with that dank odor—the one I smelled the night the feather warning was left.

"I'm right behind you," Sandi murmured, linking her finger in my belt loop.

I could hear Nick's labored breathing behind us as we inched forward on our hands and knees into the unknown. Every time I moved my hand forward, I would brace myself for something that might slither under—or strike—my palm in the dark. After what seemed like hours, I stopped.

"What?" Sandi whispered.

"Listen." There was a strange rustling ahead. I sat back on my heels. "You hear that, Nick?"

"Yeah, and do you smell that acid odor?"

"Sure do."

We held still there in the dark. It didn't sound like anything I had ever heard before.

All at once the rustling grew louder.

"Duck!" Nick shouted, his pick clanging to the rocky ground. "Cover your heads!"

I stretched out so fast I bit my lip. The throbbing started immediately. But I didn't care. I was more intent on protecting my head.

Swoosh! All at once thousands of sharp wings began beating us, smothering us. Shrill cries mingled with the whirling.

"Bats!" Nick announced in a muffled voice. "Lay low. Don't try to fight them."

I lay there, strange creatures tangling in my hair and whacking my body. But I didn't move. Again and again they hit us, dive-bombing us in waves. By now I was drawn up into a tight shell. "You okay, Sandi?" I felt like my back had become a dartboard.

"Uh-huh," she managed to utter against her knee.

After a few eternities, the attacks began to grow fewer and the air no longer screeched.

At last it was deathly still again.

"Wow, are you two okay?" I crawled back to check on them. In the beam of light, Sandi's eyes were as big as Frisbees. "If Upshan's somewhere ahead, he sure knows we're here by now."

Nick grunted. "Maybe the bats were his warning."

Sandi groaned.

"Listen, maybe you two should wait here," I said, dabbing at my swollen lip. "The river can't be far now."

"No way." It was Sandi who spoke.

So we crept on. I admit I was glad to have my friends still with me. A few feet deeper into the cave, the dripping ceiling became higher. It made me feel more in control. But the heavy dripping made the footing more treacherous. We all were clinging to the slick walls for support.

I suggested we each carry one of the picks so we could steady our footing. But when I worked back to get mine, Sandi went ahead with hers.

"You better wait, Sis," Nick called.

"Yeah, I want to lead, Sandi," I said. "I've got the light."

She didn't answer. But we could hear her footsteps growing dimmer.

"Hurry up, Nick," I urged as he tried to untangle the head of his pronged pick from mine.

But just as I got my "walking stick," we heard a bloodcurdling scream.

"Sandi!" We both ran, slipping and sliding, toward the screams. They were now pleas, *"Hurry! Hurry!"*

Just as we turned a slight corner, I pulled up short. There at the edge of my shoes were Sandi's fingers. She was dangling into an open cavern, her grip slipping fast.

"Hold my waist!" I ordered Nick. I then grabbed

both her wrists and told her not to squirm. "You got me, Nick?"

"Barely," he gasped.

"Now step backward slowly . . . slowly . . . slow . . ." And little by little we pulled Sandi free as far as her hips. It was like a deadly game of tug-of-war. Now she would be able to use her legs to help push herself up.

"Get your breath," I warned her. "Nick, you okay back there?" His breathing was labored.

"I'm okay," he managed to utter.

"Okay, Sandi," I called, tightening my grip on her wrists.

"Here goes. One . . . two . . . three."

With a gut-wrenching tug we pulled her over the rim. I then pulled her back to safer ground.

We all three collapsed like rag dolls. Nothing could be heard but our gasps and the endless dripping. I was as limp as a rope.

When I had caught my breath, I struggled to my feet and aimed the light ahead. Maybe it was my imagination, but its beam seemed dimmer. I checked its switch. It was then that I heard it—the sound of rushing water.

Or was it the sound of snakes slithering?

26

"What do you think?" Nick said, leaning on his pick.

All of us stared at the new dark crossroads that opened before us. Which one led to the River of Tears?

"I say toss for it," Sandi said. "Nick, have you got a coin?"

"No!" I protested. "This isn't some game. Our *lives* are at stake here. There's got to be a better way—a more scientific way."

Both folded their arms and looked at me. Their expressions said the ball was now in my court.

"I get it!" I moistened several fingers, then held them up to one chamber. I repeated it for the other chamber. "This one," I announced, pointing to the one on our left.

"I don't get it," Sandi said flatly.

"Me, either." Nick rested his pick on his shoulder. "But you're the boss, Brook."

"Simple. We're looking for a river, right? Well, a river means rushing water and rushing water means strong air currents." I pointed to the cave pathway I had selected. "That one definitely has the stronger airflow."

"You know what?" Nick said, his jaw slack. "I'm totally impressed."

"You should be," Sandi snapped. "That's the kind of brain power I expect from *you*, bro."

. I didn't pay any attention to Sandi's mood. I was too busy feeling and tapping along the dark, narrow corridor that led to the depths of this cave. It seemed to twist and turn endlessly. *And every step might be bringing us closer to some serpentine monster*, I thought.

Suddenly the hand I'd been running along the cold, slimy wall felt nothing. I reached farther toward the wall. "There's an opening here," I whispered. "Check it out."

Nick flicked on the ailing flashlight.

"Ohhh," breathed Sandi, obviously in awe. "How beautiful."

The room before us looked like it was made for an ice princess. Everything—the walls, the ceiling, the floors—was dripping with heavy icicles.

"Stalactites and stalagmites," Nick declared. "They are mineral deposits that collect one drop at a time."

Sandi and I ignored him as we stepped into the icy palace. Running our hands over it, we reveled in its beauty. "Oh, look," Sandi cried. "A kind of throne—or altar."

I went over for a look at the table-flat piece of white rock. On the wall behind it, I spied marks. As I got closer I realized they were drawings. They looked like a child's sketches.

Nick studied them closely. "Man, these must be as old as these mountains."

"Let me see!" Sandi tried to push her brother aside but he wouldn't move.

"Let's go." Nick turned Sandi toward the chamber's entrance. "They're nothing, really."

But I slipped in behind him. I knew him too well— he had seen something. Then I was sorry, because there on the wall was a huge snake with a mane of feathers. It was in a semicoiled position, its mouth open and fangs dripping. And before it was something like an altar or table where a human figure was strapped. Over the person's body slithered many small serpents.

"Night-Twisters!" I shouted before I caught myself.

"What?" Sandi was studying something in the corner.

Nick shushed me, motioning to his sister. I nodded in agreement. The fact that this could be Upshan's room of sacrifice would be our secret. After Sandi's near-fatal fall, she didn't need any more terror.

"Hey, you two," she said, motioning. "Come look in this corner. It looks like some big nest or something. There are even bones here. Gross!"

Nick and I exchanged glances. But we went over anyway. What could be worse than finding out you are in some ancient room of torture?

116

We soon found out.

Just as we knelt to inspect Sandi's "nest," we heard a snarl behind us. Turning quickly we saw our entrance blocked by not a snake but an enormous bear. He was standing on his back paws, his front paws flailing in our direction.

"Quick!" I shouted. "Get under something!"

We scrambled desperately for some kind of ledge or overhang that could shield us, but there was nothing. Now we knew too late whose "nest" we'd found. The bones? We didn't dare guess.

"This is it!" Sandi cried. "Nick, you've really got us in trouble now."

Nick didn't say anything. He was too busy trying to crawl back to the wall where he had left the two picks.

But the bear threatened to get there first.

"Wait!" I called. "That's it. Wait till I get his attention, then grab the picks and aim at his nose—it's his only sensitive spot."

Nick nodded, crouching in a starting position.

"No!" shouted Sandi.

But I was already sliding with my back to the wall. The reared bear looked from me to Nick. Nick wasn't moving. I was. "Not yet," I said to Nick. "Not yet . . ." The bear lowered to four paws and turned toward me. *"Now!"*

Nick grabbed both picks and came at the beast, flailing the sticks like a madman. The animal seemed confused.

117

"Run, Sandi!" I shouted. "Run!" I was reaching for a pick but Nick wouldn't let go. "I mean it, Nick," I screamed. "Let me have one!"

"Arrgh!" Nick planted a strong blow on the charging bear's snout. We watched as it turned in circles, then rolled over once, got up, and headed for the opening.

"What's he doing?" Sandi asked as we grabbed our gear.

"I don't know." I snatched a pick. "All I know is the only chance a person has against a charging bear is whacking him on the nose."

Nick's eyes brightened. "I bet I know. I bet he's headed for the river. All animals find relief from pain in water."

I slapped him on the back. "Good job. And isn't that the same river we're headed for?"

This brought a groan from both of them.

"And who's to say that bear is alone?" Sandi added. "Come on, you two. Enough is enough. I say let's try to get out of here with our lives. The entrance can't be too far."

"Are you crazy?" Nick said, blocking the entrance. "This is Brook's mission—and her and her dad's only hope."

Sandi refused to look at him. I hated to see Sandi like this. I knew she was petrified. I was, too. But Nick was right—this was my fight, not theirs. "Listen, guys, I really appreciate all you've done, but I want to go on alone. It's safer that way. Quicker, too," I added.

"See there," Nick said accusingly to his sister. "Now you're forcing Brook to try to shake us off. Proud of yourself?"

Sandi shook her brother's hands free and stepped into the corridor. "Come on. Let's get this over with. What's a giant serpent, a few million bats and rattlesnakes, and an injured bear, anyway?" She pointed to the two picks. "After all, we've always got two wooden sticks and a dying flashlight."

And with that we ventured deeper into the cave on the *kontai*.

27

"The river!" Sandi cried.

But a few feet farther we heard sloshing. Nick wanted to walk beside me, but I cautioned that single file was still the safest way.

We carefully slid down a slippery, angled rock, and there it was—a swiftly rushing river. It was so narrow in spots the current sent up spray.

I was so glad it wasn't a nest of snakes I wanted to shout.

I stood there holding the swinging beam and surveying the river.

"There!" Nick pointed to a shelflike formation on the opposite side of the wall. "That must be his ledge."

I agreed. But I was more interested in the swift current. How was I ever going to get across? After all, our footing had been terrible in the moist cave. And if I were swept away by this dark, cavernous river, where would I end up? Dashed to pieces in some deep cavern?

I looked down at the pick in my hand. Yes! And Nick's pick had an even longer handle.

I quickly told them my plan. Both Sandi and Nick were hesitant. But I knew what would convince them. "Listen, you two," I reminded them. "That monster snake isn't going to stay away forever. This is his home. So it's now or never, right?"

"I don't like the odds," Sandi grumbled.

"Who does?" Nick answered. "But Brook's right. And it's a long way back."

So we began to plot my course.

"Easy," Nick said as I edged out into the dark water. After testing several launching areas, I had decided not to select a narrow crossing, but one wider and more shallow. This way the current might not sweep me away.

I hoped.

By the time I had waded out to my waist, I felt numb. The water was icy and, even worse, the footing began to drop off. But there was no way out. *Okay, here goes everything.* By now I was only a few feet from the other side. "Okay, ready."

Nick waded into the shallows. "Man, this is freezing." He extended the shaft of the longest pick toward me. Holding the pick itself, he made sure Sandi was holding on to him. With her free hand, she grasped a chink in the rocky wall. "You got me?" he called behind.

"I think so," Sandi answered.

"Don't think. Know." His voice was tight.

By now I was swimming, one-armed, toward the ledge, still holding the shaft. I grasped the stone in my free hand. Although the water was frigid, the current was not as swift as it looked from up on the rock.

I was now right in front of the ledge. Thank goodness, it was a low shelf of rock. With my free hand I managed to grasp the stone firmly, then I gave the weird rock my best softball underhanded pitch. *Please, Lord,* I prayed silently, *let it land.*

KLUNK.

I held my breath. It rocked back and forth a little.

"Oh, no!" yelled Sandi somewhere behind me.

Then the stone grew still.

"Yea!" Nick and Sandi shouted. But I didn't react. I was too busy pulling myself back to safety on the pick shaft.

"Way to go!" Nick patted my shoulder as we waded back to where Sandi was. "Here. Warm up in this." He slid his jacket over my shoulders.

I was too exhausted to thank him. Sinking to my knees, I knelt there, gasping. But over and over I kept thanking God silently.

"You okay?" Sandi put her hand on my back.

I nodded.

"But you're shivering." She helped me put my arms into Nick's jacket.

"Thanks," I managed weakly. At least by now I was

able to stand. But my hands were almost numb, so I rammed them into the pockets of Nick's jacket. Down in the recess of one, I felt something. Taking it out, I studied it under the weakening beam.

Then I really grew numb. Down-to-my-toes numb. I looked at the object, then at Nick and Sandi. No! I wanted to scream. No!

28

All at once my whole world caved in on me. Here in the depths of this cave, I began to put together certain missing pieces in the revenge of Upshan.

Play it cool, I urged myself, as I tried to clear my throat. "We better get going," I advised. "It's a long way back to home base."

They quickly agreed. "Besides, we could meet him on our way back," Nick added.

"You think?" I was already slip-sliding up the rocky path. "Boy, I hope so."

"What?" Sandi cried. "Are you crazy?"

"Not anymore," I answered in a firm voice.

"Leave her alone," Nick whispered behind me. "It's her confidence talking."

I had to smile at the thought. Did he ever have a surprise in store!

When we got back to the entrance, the sun was beginning to set. By now we were not only cold and wet but hungry, too. Clinging to cliffs and bushes, we rappelled our way off the ledge down to the path leading to Nick's truck.

"Let's go to our house," Sandi suggested. "We can dry off and celebrate. 'Death to death stalking' let's call it."

Nick seconded that, but I nixed it. "No, I want you two over at my place. Dad'll be home soon."

"But why?" Nick asked as he started the motor. "Are you going to tell him?"

"Something like that," I said whimsically, resting my head on the back of the seat.

Sandi said I was certainly in a strange mood. But I didn't respond. I just watched the sunset over the mountains.

Once we got back to our chalet, I gave Nick some of Dad's dry clothes and offered Sandi some of mine. Neither of them seemed interested as I built a fire. They were more interested in my strange mood.

I then reached into the pocket of Nick's jacket and clasped the object I had discovered earlier. "Why did you two set me up this way?"

Nick turned from the fire. "Set you up? I don't get it."

"All this talk about Upshan was your game, wasn't it? The cursed mountain, the snakes, death stalking, everything."

They looked at each other. But it was a look of suspicion, not surprise.

"Brook, what's gotten into you?" Sandi stepped toward me, but I stepped back.

I held out the dark stone in my hand. It looked like "my" lightning stone—only this one was missing the smooth crystalline surface. Tiny phosphorescent lights twinkled in the crudely made object. "Was this the trial run before you perfected mine?" I threw the fake stone on the hearth.

Sandi swung toward her brother. "You said you got rid of that thing days ago."

Nick cringed. Silently he turned to stare into the crackling fire.

"But why?" My voice was more pleading than demanding.

Sandi would not meet my gaze. "Dad heard from the rental people your dad was a lawyer. So he said you had to be a scout for some big resort corporation. Then my brother said he had just the plan to scare anyone off this mountain forever."

"But Dad's just studying to be a lawyer."

"My dad didn't buy that. The government's going to sell off this whole mountain soon. It's a big secret now. So Dad's company wants to bid for it first . . . for a big resort. He figured your dad's company had gotten wind of the sale, too."

"You mean you planted those rattlesnakes, the door carving, the lightning stone, the feather, even that snake pit?"

Nick nodded weakly, never turning from the fire.

126

"Those snakes weren't really rattlesnakes. That's what *you* believed. The ones I planted in your room and in the pit were garter snakes. They're nonpoisonous. When they're alarmed, they often coil up and flatten their heads like pit vipers. It's called mimicry. But if you knew much about snakes, you would have known the difference. I didn't want to hurt you, I just wanted to scare you away. When you thought it was a rattlesnake you saw, it made the scheme work even better."

"He's telling the truth, Brook. We never took you to the shed behind the trailer. That's where Nick keeps his snakes, mostly garter snakes, but he has one big boa. That's the one he planted outside your window the night he trashed your cabin."

I had to sit down. Too many questions were swirling in my brain. "And you put that hideous tattoo on my poor Brat? But what about the dye without pigmentation?"

"Simple," Nick answered in a low voice. "It came from the mountain cassia plant. The veterinarian must not know much about mountain herbs."

"And the loud crunching noise following us through the woods the day the trooper came, and . . . and that night the feather was left?"

Sandi stole a glance at me. "All Nick."

"But, Brook, my dad didn't have anything to do with this," Nick said. "It was my idea, and Sandi reluctantly went along with it. You see, Dad's been so sad ever since Mom died, and when he got worried about losing the deal on the mountain land, well . . . I just wanted to do something to help him. When you heard him tell me 'You were right, I got too close,' he was talking about the loose rock on the ledges. I always warned him he was stepping too close to the ledges, and he could fall. But when he said that in the hospital, I knew it would play along with our story, so I whispered that line about his accident proving the legend was true loud enough so you would hear it."

"But hey!" I stood up. "What about Sister Howling Wind? Don't tell me she was in on this scheme, too."

"No," Sandi assured me.

"But what about her story about Upshan killing the people in her village? Even those old books at the library said they died mysteriously."

Nick turned to face me for the first time. "'Old' is the word. The books were out-of-date. The truth was, her village was the victim of a government experiment gone wrong. Our military was secretly experimenting with poisonous gases up in the mountains. It was before World War II. And, well, the wind changed, you might say."

"How do you know that?"

"I can show you copies of the investigation. It was hushed up until just recently, when it was published in a few military journals. But old people like Sister seldom accept the truth. I heard she doesn't even believe in such things as poisonous gas."

I didn't find that consoling. Here I was having believed in a giant mythical serpent who had marked Dad and me for death. Where did I go wrong? My eyes began to sting.

"You know the worst part of this whole thing?" Sandi said as she swung around to face me. "For me it was liking you. I hadn't planned on that when I promised to go along. Then—and I don't expect you to believe this—then I wanted out. Ask Nick."

"She's right," Nick said. "But I put her on a guilt trip."

"And you know the strangest part?" She didn't wait for me to respond. "What I liked best about you was the way you reminded me of my mom." She sniffed slightly. "I mean, she was a good person, too." She met my gaze. "I hope we can be friends again."

"You still have to tell Dad. He deserves that much."

"Sure, sure. But you mean we still might be friends again someday?"

I looked at her hopeful face. "Anything's possible. After all, you two didn't know it . . . but you did give me the most exciting summer of my life."

And with that, the three of us gathered by the fire, silently warming ourselves by the light.

1

It was another new house and another new town. I was getting used to having a new bedroom and attending a new school and a new church every year or two.

Dad worked for a big company with offices nation-wide. He did well there. His boss valued him. He transferred Dad to wherever the company was having trouble. This time it was Riverdale.

I liked the new house. My room here was bigger than my rooms in any of the other houses we had lived in. The room next to mine was my brother Tommy's nursery. Dad and Mom's room was down a long hall-way from my room.

Dad had already put my sign on my bedroom door. It told everyone this was MAX'S ROOM. I was named after my dad. He is Maxwell Walker and so am I. Mom calls him Maxie. She didn't like the name "Junior" or "Little Maxie," though. She decided to call me Max. Dad calls me Buddy. I like that. It makes me feel very close to him.

It was Saturday and I was busy unpacking boxes. I

removed my baseball card collection from one of the boxes and placed it on the bookshelf in my bedroom. I had some great cards. Dad had been collecting for years, and he gave me his collection. I was the only kid I knew with a Mickey Mantle and a Hank Aaron. Dad was great about helping me find the best cards.

When I finished the cards, I grabbed the box with my books in it. My favorite set was The Chronicles of Narnia by C. S. Lewis. Mom read them to me when I was young, but I went through them again. They were really interesting. As I stacked my books on the bed, our dog, Snowball, padded into the room.

Snowball was a white puff of fur. When we had talked about getting a dog I had wanted a big dog. But Mom said because we moved so much and might not always have a fenced backyard, we should get a small dog that we could keep in the house. So we got Snowball, a bichon frise. He's small, and he's my best friend.

Just like Dad called me Buddy, I called Snowball Buddy. It made him sound tougher. One look at him and people knew that he wasn't tough at all.

Snowball jumped on the bed and knocked over the stack of books. They went all over the floor.

"Buddy, get off the bed. I'm working here," I scolded.

He just looked at me and tilted his head from side to side, listening to me. I sometimes thought he understood what I said to him. This time, though, he didn't care if I needed to put away my books. He wanted to play. To be honest, that was what I wanted to do as well.

I placed my forearms on the bed. I once saw a TV show that said this position was the international dog sign that meant "play." He imitated me then jumped off the bed and ran down the stairs. I was in hot pursuit.

I followed Snowball into the family room where Mom and Dad were busy unpacking boxes.

Dad glanced up at me. "How's your unpacking coming, Buddy?"

"It was going pretty good. That is, until Snowball decided to 'help' me. He scattered my books all over the place."

Mom laughed. She called Snowball over to her and rubbed him behind his ears. "Poor Snowball. None of us have paid much attention to him today, what with all this unpacking."

Snowball wagged his tail as Mom scratched him under his chin.

"Max, will you please take that box to the attic for me?" Mom pointed to some boxes in the corner of the room. "The one marked Christmas decorations. I don't think we have room for it in any of the closets."

"Sure thing, Mom." I picked up the box. "Come on, Buddy. You can go with me."

Snowball scampered behind me as I carried the box to the attic steps.

The stairs to the attic were dark and creaky. Each

one I climbed sounded like it was saying back to me, "Get off. I'm old. I hurt when you walk on me."

Of course, that was just my imagination. My parents thought I had an overactive imagination. When I was a little kid I thought there were monsters in my bedroom. Before going to sleep at night I always asked Mom and Dad to look under my bed and in my closet. They always assured me there were no monsters hiding in my room.

I had the feeling that my new house would have plenty of things in it that would engage my imagination. After all, it was a big house with lots of rooms to explore.

As I climbed the attic stairs, I heard a noise. I stopped and listened. *That was not my imagination.*

I moved up another stair and held by breath to listen. I heard it again. A rush of fear prickled my skin. Something was in the attic.

2

I thought of going down to get Dad, but then he might think it was me imagining things again. Dad thought it was something that I ate that caused my imagination to go into overdrive. He would always say, "You better cut down on the pizza with extra creeps."

I had to explore this one myself. Besides, I had my trusty and faithful protector and sidekick with me.

Or so I thought.

I looked around for Snowball. He wasn't behind me. Apparently he had found something more interesting to do.

I thought about calling him, but I did not want to make any noise that might scare away the intruder before I could catch him, her, or it. I was not sure why I thought I should or could catch whatever was in our attic.

I took another step and listened. The intruder must have heard me. A crashing sound sent chills up my spine. The thing in our attic must have moved quickly and broken something. I wasn't sure I should go any farther, but I wasn't going to be a fraidy cat either.

I took another step. I was high enough to see into the attic. I had hoped that the sunlight would be shining into the attic. From where I stood I could see that the windows were so dirty that very little sunlight could filter through.

I glanced around the dimly lit attic, but I did not see any sign of the intruder. What really had me worried was how I was going to get into the attic without the intruder seeing me. I had to be prepared.

I saw an old piece of wood lying on the attic floor. If I could get to the wood then I would have something I could use to defend myself.

The noise distracted me again. It was like a great whistling or the sound of wind in a horrible thunderstorm. I had to make my move. I tried to remember everything I had ever seen in those karate movies.

I jumped up to the top stair. I set the box on the floor then dived toward the piece of wood. My body slammed against the exposed wood in the slanted attic wall. It hurt, but I was able to grab my protection device.

I could make out a few shapes in the darkness. They appeared to be old trunks. The former owners must have left them here when they moved. I imagined they were filled with great stuff to play with. Maybe some old pirate put a treasure map in one of them. I made a mental note to come back up here with a flashlight.

I slowly crawled toward one of the shapes. It was a large storage trunk. I hid behind it.

I took a deep breath and looked around the side of the trunk.

Someone was standing about three feet from me.

SPINE CHILLERS™

Max doesn't mind moving because his mom
always buys pizza with extra cheese
for every meal until they
are settled in. His dad is sure the cheese is
causing Max's imagination to work overtime
when Max starts seeing and
hearing strange things.
But Max isn't so sure, and neither
are his friends who spend the night
at his house.

It's too late to say no thanks to seconds in . . .

Pizza with Extra Creeps

SpineChillers™ #4
by Fred E. Katz